POLITE SOCIETY

POLITE SOCIETY

MELANIE SUMNER

HOUGHTON MIFFLIN

Boston   New York

1995

Copyright © 1995 by Melanie Sumner

For information about permission to reproduce selections from
this book, write to Permissions, Houghton Mifflin Company,
215 Park Avenue South, New York, New York 10003.

Library of Congress Cataloging-in-Publication Data

Sumner, Melanie.
Polite Society / Melanie Sumner.
p.   cm.
I S B N 0-395-68998-8
I. Title.
PS3569.U46P6   1995
813'.54 — dc20   94-41324   CIP

Book design by Anne Chalmers

Printed in the United States of America

QUM 10 9 8 7 6 5 4 3 2 1

Portions of this book have appeared, in different form,
in *The New Yorker, Story,* and *New Stories from
the South* (Algonquin Books, 1994).

TO MOM AND DAD

AND MAX

ACKNOWLEDGMENTS

I am grateful to the late Seymour Lawrence, who fought for this book from a hospital bed. I am grateful to my editor, Hilary Liftin, who understood this book and knew exactly how to edit it. I am grateful to my parents for giving me money to write this book. I am grateful to Yaddo and The Fine Arts Work Center for giving me time and space to write this book. I am grateful to *The New Yorker* for publishing parts of this book, and especially to Linda Asher, who made me a tougher writer and taught me how to catch a cab in New York City. I am grateful to Shannon Ravenel for telling me that first books are sexy so I should take my time, and for publishing part of this book in *New Stories from the South*. I am grateful to Lois Rosenthal for publishing parts of this book in *Story*. I am grateful to the United States Peace Corps for sending me to Senegal, where I found the stories for this book. I am grateful to Ousmane Sané for taking me to the *marabout* who made the *gris-gris* for this book. I am grateful to Leigh Swigart, who taught me how to catch a cab in Dakar and who patiently deciphered the Wolof in this book. I am grateful to Georges Borchardt, who deciphered the French in this book. I am grateful to my teacher Leslie Epstein, who made me a better Southerner and taught me not to write a sentimental book. I am grateful to my teacher Max Steele, who taught me how to love my characters and how to tell the truth, and allowed me to read him this book over the telephone. I am grateful to Brad Gioia, my high school English teacher, who allowed me to write short stories instead of essays. I am grateful to God, Deb Manangelus, Donna Brooks, Gretchen Mattox, Billie Jean Mann, Karie Grazier, Richard McCann, and Charlie Thomas for teaching me how to stay alive so I could write this book. I am grateful to Leonard Smith, who laughed at this book and suggested I name it *Polite Society.*

CONTENTS

POLITE SOCIETY

THE EDGE OF THE SKY

"Someone in your house will be unfaithful," said the *seetkat*. Her black skin was so wrinkled that it looked as if life had wadded her up like a paper bag and then, in random acts of grace, tried to smooth her out again. She was no bigger than the child sleeping beside her on the bed. Mumbling incantations, she rattled the cowrie shells in her bony hand and tossed them across the faded blanket, where they formed the blurred outline of a fish. Thea, the wife of the American ambassador to Senegal, and her maid, Coumba, leaned forward to study the mysterious shape of their futures.

The old witch said something in Wolof to Coumba, who replied "Waaw, waaw" in assent and leaned back, adjusting the bright yellow robe that slid off one glossy black shoulder. She was tall and slender with an exquisite face. As she turned her head, fine black braids weighted with metal beads clacked softly against her neck. "Ndeysaan," she said in sympathy, and smiled. Her gums had been dyed blue to make her teeth dazzle. Sitting next to her maid, Thea felt like a pasty white ball of dough. She wore a practical, mud-colored skirt and a dowdy blouse. Her bangs were cut too short.

Translating the *seetkat*'s prescription, Coumba told Thea in French, "You buy three white birds. Let one go west in the leaving sun, let one go east in the coming sun, and let one go where it will. You buy four meters of black cloth and give them to a beggar. You put three eggs in the sea. God will know."

"Isn't this interesting," said Thea, planning a visit to her tailor.

In the dirt yard of the dilapidated house, two boys with quick eyes and long, dusty legs edged shyly back from the baby blue Lincoln Continental to let the ambassador's wife and her maid pass by them. Samba, the chauffeur, stepped out in his blue uniform with the gold braid and opened the doors. Leaning back in the cool leather seat, Thea considered the witch's prophecy. Did Grant have a lover?

On the Avenue Lamine Gueye, at the hand-lettered sign ELI-MANE COUTURE, MAÎTRE TAILLEUR, Samba parked the car and walked around to open Thea's door. Without looking back at him, she stepped toward the rusty gate, where she was immediately surrounded by two boys and a leper, all clamoring for money. "Shoo!" she said, clutching her Gucci bag to her breast. "Shoo! Shoo!" Then she turned back to the car and called, "Coumba!"

The regal maid appeared. "Bàyyil madame!" she ordered the children. "Your father will beat you!" They scattered. She and the leper exchanged a few words about the manners of children today, and then she set a coin in his stump of a hand and followed her mistress into the courtyard.

"Asalaa maalekum!" Thea called in the doorway.

"Maalekum salaam!" replied three lanky boys working the treadles of their antique black sewing machines.

From the shadowy depths of the room, behind a white electric Singer, Elimane Couture, Master Tailor, rose to his feet. "Bonjour, Madame Ambassadeur, ça va? Ça va, ça va? Bien, bien, assieds-toi." He was a thin, handsome man who smiled constantly. His voice rolled out smooth and somnolent, and his eyes were half-shut, like a crocodile's.

They shook hands and he seated her in a metal folding chair, sending one of his assistants out for Cokes and cigarettes. He merely nodded to Coumba, who stood next to her mistress, contemplating the outfits hanging along the dark pink walls. "You are here," said Elimane. "Are you in peace? Peace only. How is Monsieur l'Ambassadeur? Bien, bien."

The boy returned, and passed out bottles of warm Coke, keeping his head down. "Qu'est-ce que tu désires aujourd'hui, Madame?" asked Elimane, smiling, lighting a cigarette. They used the familiar *tu* with each other, but, either because he couldn't pronounce Thea or because he never tired of playing with the women who came to him to be dressed, he called her Madame. She called him Elimane Couture, the label he sewed into the backs of her clothes.

"What do I desire," Thea asked herself, flipping through the Paris *Vogue* he handed her. She turned the slick pages of emaciated women with melon breasts and chilled eyes and then closed the magazine and leaned forward, resting her chin in her hands. "I desire to be twenty years old, gorgeous, and . . . reckless." Their eyes met.

"Ah, bon."

"Saay-saay nga," suggested Coumba. She laughed with Elimane and the boys and then smiled impishly and folded her hands in her lap.

Thea thought that *saay-saay* meant horny, but was afraid to ask. Coumba was probably jealous because she had given the witch a ten thousand C.F.A. note. Thea cleared her throat. "Make me another little black dress, Elimane. Round neck, pearl buttons — you know. Maybe we'll try an A-line to hide my hips."

"Oui, Madame." Drawing on his cigarette, he bent his head down to sketch the dress on a scrap of paper. As usual, he ignored her instructions. "It's red," he explained. "Silk or satin, as you like. Okay, ça va?"

"Non, ça ne va pas."

"Ça va, ça va. Bien, bien." Pulling a tape around his neck, he led her into the curtained corner of the room, to be measured. When he knelt down to measure the hem, she looked over his shoulders to her own image in the streaked mirror. She was tall, and twelve pounds overweight. A new hairdresser had scalped her, leaving only a down of dark feathers on her head. Fine lines spread out from her eyes and mouth like back roads on a map. "Oh, Elimane," she said. "Fix me."

"Don't move. This must fit perfectly." As he adjusted the metal tip of the tape just above her kneecap, his fingers streamed across her calf. She closed her eyes and was a child again, standing rigidly, with an aching neck, while her mother knelt at her feet with her mouth full of pins. Thea's nose began to itch, and then an ear, and then her leg. "Relax your shoulders," said Elimane. She wondered what the assistants — cousins, he called them — thought when they saw his white tennis shoes and her black flats under the curtain. "Buy red silk, Madame," he said, opening the curtain.

At cocktail hour, Thea looked at Grant as though she were some other woman, trying to steal an ambassador. He was forty years old, three years older than she, a big, restless man with thick eyebrows and deep blue eyes. His large nose made him look friendly. He had a Harvard accent.

"How was your trip?" she asked, crossing her legs.

"It was a complete failure." He rattled the ice in his glass. "Michael Jackson gave us all some comic relief, though. He wore a surgical mask. He had some fabulous fear of being contaminated by the air in Côte d'Ivoire, but the Africans didn't understand. They were divided between wondering if they smelled bad and wondering if he were dying of AIDS and didn't want to infect them. One of the government ministers, a huge Muslim who has just turned Catholic and can't hold his liquor, said to him, 'You don't need all these bodyguards; we wouldn't sell a man into slavery twice.'" Thea started to say something, but Grant interrupted her. "An adviser tried to hush him up, but the minister said, 'No, no, I speak the truth. He is neither black nor white, neither man nor woman; who would buy this creature?'"

Coumba came to the door and curtsied to Grant. "Bonsoir, Coumba," he said sweetly, gazing up and down her body. "Tu es très belle ce soir." Thea's throat constricted. She pulled her bangs down.

"Grant, I'd like another olive." Appalled at the bitterness in her voice, she added, "Please." Grant was practicing his Wolof with Coumba. He had become fairly quick with it; they were laughing at a joke. Thea didn't understand a word. She rose so they could see that she intended to get her own olive.

"No, darling, sit down," said Grant. "I'll get it for you." When Thea made a face, he raised his eyebrows. "Shall we ask Coumba to put the steaks on the grill now, or would you rather wait a few moments?"

"Now. You're hungry." When they were alone, she peered into his face as if she had lost something there. Seeing his hand on another woman would be as horrifying as watching another hand sign her own name in her own handwriting.

"What is it?"

"Kiss me." Obediently, he gave her a peck.

"No, Grant. Kiss me."

"Honey, I'm tired."

"Are you?"

They dined at opposite ends of a long table spread with a starched white cloth. Two white candles burned in silver candlesticks. Thea lifted a succulent bit of pink beef on a silver fork. It tasted like ash. This was the fifth year of their marriage.

"Thea," Grant said. She knew the tones of his voice as if they were bells. Each one signified an argument that they had pulled between them until the words rubbed off, leaving only the hollow ring of the chime.

"Grant," she answered.

In the morning Thea blew the dust off her Jane Fonda video and got down on the floor in front of the TV. From the doorway, Coumba watched in amazement as her mistress did sit-ups. When Thea began to scissor her legs in the air, the maid wailed, "Madame, your face is turning red. Stop! You'll hurt yourself!" She tried to distract Thea. "What time is it?" she asked. "Should I make lemon chicken or garlic chicken?"

"Twenty-one, damn you, twenty-three . . ." said Thea, grunting.

That afternoon they went to the largest cloth shop in Dakar, a two-story building crammed with bolts of cream taffeta, deepwater velvet, and sunset satins, run by a Lebanese family with gold eyes.

"The beige silk chiffon," said Thea. Coumba flicked the tip of her tongue out the side of her mouth to point to the bolt of red silk. Thea moaned. "Don't help."

"If I were white I think I would wear red."

"This one?" asked the boy. "This red one?" He slit his golden eyes as if they had just found the single treasured item in the store, the one the family had hoped to keep for themselves. "This silk is woven by hand." As he lifted the bolt, his prune-faced grandmother removed the pin, and the silk ran like blood over Thea's open hand.

Coumba started the bargaining. "Four thousand C.F.A."

The boy and the grandmother laughed. The grandmother let the silk slide through her gnarled fingers, dipping it out to catch the light. "Eight thousand," said the boy.

"Forty-two hundred," offered Coumba. The man appeared insulted. They waited.

"Sixty-two hundred," he said. "That's my final price."

At this audacious suggestion, Coumba covered her mouth with her hand. Then she stiffened her back and looked away, preparing to haggle again.

"Never mind!" said Thea, taking out her wallet to pay him. With a pair of scissors, the old woman cut the silk in a rip.

Samba, the chauffeur, had gone across the street to the mosque, taking a mat he kept rolled up in the trunk. The pair of Nikes Grant had given him sat in a row of plastic flip-flops outside the tiled arches. Samba had told a small boy in ragged shorts to guard the car, and the child was washing it with a bucket of brown water. Thea looked past him to the mosque, at the rows of women kneeling outside, fumbling with long strings of beads, and beyond them to the shadowy interior, where she made out the pink soles of praying men. She imagined tearing off her clothes and running in there. Immediately she glanced away. The boy was tenderly wiping a dirty rag across the reflection of his face in the chrome.

On the drive back to Elimane Couture, Samba chastised Coumba for not praying. As she bantered with him, she tugged her robe over her shoulders, rolled her eyes, and flashed her blue gums. Thea could not understand much Wolof; she decided to leave them in the car. In the shadowy room, resonant with the rhythmic treadling of the machines, she clutched the brown paper parcel under one arm and shook hands with the line of assistants, working her way up to Elimane. "Here. It's red," she said, shifting her weight on her feet.

"Ah, bon. Ça va, toi?" Slowly he untied the bundle, putting the string into a box. "Ça va bien?" He stood directly under the light bulb, folding the cloth into lengths over his outstretched arm to make sure the Lebanese hadn't cheated her. In the dim light the silk waved and shimmered.

"It's a sin to cut it," said Thea.

"I'll sew it with sequins," said Elimane, folding it back into a square, "so that you will be like a fish, catching every color, and everyone will try to catch you." He moved his hand like a fish swimming. "When you want to be red you stand in the direct light, and no one will touch you."

"I don't think I want sequins. How much will this cost?"

"You'll have some tea?"

"No," she said, twisting her fingers in her bangs. "Give me a price."

"We are friends." He smiled, showing his white teeth. "You have no faith in me?"

During the drive home she recalled a Wolof proverb: "If you chase two rabbits, you will catch nothing." For a moment she thought that Samba was talking to Coumba about her.

The next thing you know, I'll be throwing eggs into the ocean, she told herself. She looked out the window at brightly painted wooden pirogues dotting the waves. The fishermen wore tangles of tiny leather *gris-gris* around their arms and waists, and tucked others inside their canoes, believing that this would keep them from drowning. Most of them could not swim. Along the corniche, the waves broke furiously against the black volcanic rock, spraying glistening arcs high into the sky.

At home Coumba began talking about babies. She was ironing, sweeping her strong, slender arm across a sheet with the grace and deliberation of a ballerina. Puffs of steam rose around her wrist, and the smell of clean cotton mingled with her own spicy fragrance. In her opinion, Madame needed a baby.

"I don't want a baby," said Thea. "I want the love of a man."

"You should have a baby."

"Who wants a baby?"

"My new husband wants a baby," said Coumba. "I say, *non, non, non.* I have six children, each one living in a different village, and I am in Dakar. You have a baby, and then you have no money. Then you have another baby. Then you have no money and you are tired all the time. Look." Setting down the iron, she lifted her blue cotton *boubou* over her firm young hips to show Thea her shriveled breasts and sagging belly.

"Will he take another wife?"

"He is saving up money for one because he wants a baby. He says I am using *maraboutage* against him, to be barren." She stared righteously at the wall. "My husband never gives me money. What good is a man who doesn't give you money? Then he asks me for money. Ask the wife for money? Laaylaay!"

"So why should I have a baby?" asked Thea.

Smiling, the maid nosed the iron around the corner of a pillowcase. "Then Coumba will have a white baby."

The steaming kitchen became unbearable. Thea wiped the bangs from her forehead with the back of her hand and then she went to the freezer and took one of the Fudgesicles that had been shipped over with tons of other American delicacies to the embassy commissary. Licking the melting chocolate, she wandered through the bare white rooms of the mansion, looking for her husband. He was in the shower, singing a rap song:

> I'm too sexy for my hat,
> I'm too sexy for my cat,
> I'm too sexy for you, baby.

The chocolate melted across her fingers and she threw the Fudgesicle into the wastebasket. With a towel she wiped her hands clean and then wiped a clear circle in the foggy mirror. Sucking in the thick steam, she said, "Grant?"

He stuck his wet head around the plastic curtain. "Meow!"

"What if Coumba were to get pregnant?"

"Then she would have a baby, eh?"

"She already has six children she can't even afford to bring to Dakar."

He shut off the water and flung back the curtain, stepping out on the bathmat. When she handed him a towel, he slapped her lightly with it. "Aren't you pretty!" With his head bent, vigorously rubbing his hair dry, he said, "Poor Coumba. Elle est très intelligente, mais elle fait l'amour sénégalaisement."

"How do you know how the Senegalese make love?"

"Because they do everything the same way: sénégalaisement." He lifted one foot to dry it with the towel. "'Oh, I'm just a possum in the road. I know what I'm doing. Here comes a big bus, far away — or is it a Peugeot up close? Only God knows. Time for a cigarette. Ho hum. I'm just a smart old possum in the road. Ho. Ho. All the time in the world.'"

"Is that your report, Mr. Ambassador?" She knelt down and pulled the towel from his hands, gently wiped his other foot dry and kissed it. She made a vague resolution to be a better wife to her husband and a better ambassador of the United States, and even considered canceling the dress.

She was standing barefoot on the concrete floor, under the flickering light bulb, in the red dress. Elimane had asked her to remove the shoes. "If you don't mind," he said, as though her body were now his property. The red silk, weighted with sequins, was cut in a simple chemise with short sleeves and ended just above her knees. As she slid the dress over her head, she sucked in her breath. He had sewn the sequins on by hand — three thousand and thirty-three of them, he assured her. They flashed in the dim room like fireflies, glittering across the floor, dotting the cheap cotton prints and plain brown wools under the needles of the sewing machines, flashing like minuscule stars on the wiry black arms of the assistants. When Elimane wiped his face with his hand, a sequin stuck to his nose. On the dress they were like scales, flickering from green to blue to yellow as Thea moved under the light, turning the red silk from dark pink to deep blue.

"I feel as though I should slither across the floor and bite something," said Thea. "I can't possibly wear this." In the corner of the room, with the curtain open, she turned slowly before the mirror, watching the red scales slide over her body and shimmer. The men watched her.

"Madame," said Elimane, "tu es belle." He sent two of the boys to the house next door, and the other one to the courtyard to make Chinese gunpowder tea.

When they were alone, he seated himself calmly behind his desk, studying the dress on her body, then lit a cigarette. "You will come to the Kilimanjaro Club with me," he said. "First we'll have dinner, then we'll dance. This is a dress for dancing."

"No," she said.

"And why not?" He smiled, graciously covering her bad manners. The Senegalese were never so tactless as to decline an invitation. They accepted, with enthusiasm, and either arrived or did not.

Thea began to sweat in the cool silk. If she said, "Because I'm married," then he would act as though she had misread his meaning, as though *she* were the one considering *him* as a potential lover. On the other hand, if she acted as though it were normal for him to ask her for a date, he would ask again. His glossy black face was as still as the ebony masks sold on the street. His eyes shifted, and she felt the full strength of his cunning.

"Ça va?" he asked. "Cigarette?"

"Ça va."

Although she hadn't smoked since college, she took the cigarette he offered and allowed him to light it. She drew on it briefly.

"You are like your Mr. Clinton — you smoke but you don't inhale, *n'est-ce pas?*" Then he asked her for a visa to the United States. "Of course, if it's inconvenient . . ." He added, "I have many friends in the American embassy."

Coumba loved the dress. She watched with silent concentration as Thea walked up and down the living room, turning slowly by the bright lamp and then by the dim one, to demonstrate how the colors changed. "Laaylaay!" Coumba said. "Give it to me."

Grant was less enthusiastic. "How much did it cost?" he asked, half joking.

"I don't know." Thea was lifting one leg in front of the mirror, admiring the slide of the scales along her hips.

"Excuse me?"

Licking her fingertips to brush her eyebrows, she said, "We haven't discussed the price yet. He suggested a visa, but I'll bargain him down."

"Sometimes I think you forget that as my wife you play a political role in this country. We don't pay for clothes with visas to the U.S."

"You don't like it," she said. "It makes me look fat. I look ridiculous. Just say so. You won't hurt my feelings." She glared at him.

"Honey, it's gorgeous. You're gorgeous." He put his arms around her, running his hand down the dress. "It's kind of scratchy though." Thea leaned back against his arms. "Just kidding," he said. "It's beautiful." With his hands on her shoulders he turned her around to unzip it. "Where are you going to wear it?"

"To the dinner for the new Japanese ambassador, what's his name?"

"Oh," said Grant.

At the dinner she sat between a U.S.A.I.D. man from Portland, named Portland, and Grant, who sat across from Portland's daughter, an eighteen-year-old who had the features of a Barbie doll with skin as smooth as plastic. Her hair was bleached, cut, and permed into a yellow mane, giving a hint of savagery to her baby face. As she talked about her sorority back in Portland, Thea watched Grant watch the girl's breasts swell softly over the white eyelet lace of her dress. Thea, in her flaming red sheath, felt like a showgirl working the table for tips. "I don't really know what I'm going to *do* with my life yet," Barbie Doll was saying, dead serious. "I mean, there are a lot of things that interest me, but, like, do I want to *do* them?"

"Some people do things, and some people fly into glass like birds." Thea had no idea why she said that. Grant kicked her foot under the table. Everyone was looking at her. Portland apparently found it amusing: he howled, which either insulted or embarrassed his daughter, who excused herself from the table.

As she walked away from them, her round, tight ass rolled under the thin white dress. Thea stared at the back of her husband's head until he turned to her again.

"Hi," he said, and smiled politely. She looked through his face as though it were a fishbowl, imagining that she watched a single goldfish swimming around a miniature treasure chest, methodically trying to escape. She saw that he was going to tell a joke. Counting his drinks, four gin and tonics, she decided that it would be in poor taste but not raunchy. Motioning to the waiter for another glass of wine, she looked along the table of Japanese and wondered how people with such trenchant minds could have such a blast at a party. One of them glanced at her dress and smiled, nodding approvingly. When she waved she felt the weight of Grant's ring on her finger.

"So he asks his wife," Grant was saying, "'Am I a *great* lover, or an *excellent* lover?'"

Later, Thea could not remember exactly when she switched to Scotch, or how she and Kiichi, the one who had nodded, ended up arm in arm, circulating through the party speaking a French they had invented themselves. Kiichi translated the French growl into "Errh, errh" and they bumped through the rooms, saying "Errh, errh" whenever they felt threatened.

When Grant found them at the end of the bar, Thea was teaching Kiichi "The Yellow Rose of Texas" in their new language.

"Honey, I think it's time to get you home," said Grant.

"Errh," said Thea.

"Errh, errh," said Kiichi. Looking at Grant's stern face, they burst into laughter.

"Stopois toi," Thea shouted to her new friend, and they both coughed and choked, trying to be serious, but just when it seemed that one of them might manage an intelligent sound, the other lapsed into a fit of giggling, and they were off again. Vaguely, Thea remembered making some joke about Grant's nose.

Gripping her arm, Grant pulled her outside and maneuvered her into the waiting Lincoln. From the back seat Thea studied the chauffeur's cap for a moment before she leaned forward, removed it from his head, and settled it on her own. He didn't turn around, but she found the set of his shoulders insulting.

"Grant, let's fire Samba and get a new chauffeur," she said in French. "I don't like him." With an apology and some reference to a malaria fever, Grant handed the hat back to the driver. Thea began to cry. Grant rested his hand on the back of her neck and pulled her ear to his mouth, whispering in English, "Would you please shut up?"

"Xala, xala, xala," Thea said loudly, intoning a curse that Wolof women put on unfaithful husbands to make them impotent.

"Fine," said Grant. He sighed and leaned back in his seat, away from his wife. "Go ahead. Ruin my career. See if you can do it in the next five minutes."

A gray light seeped under the curtains. Inside Thea's head, in the soft, dark center, a talon clawed, systematically ripping the delicate tissues of her brain into ribbons of pain. "Grant!" she croaked, digging her face into his back. Her swollen tongue scraped against the rough lining of her mouth, making her words thick. "Grant, I'm sorry. Please help me, Grant." With the most profound hatred she had ever known, she hated herself. "Grant?" she begged.

Without answering, he rolled out of bed and went to the shower. When he was dressed, he leaned over the bed, filling her nostrils with the crisp scent of after-shave. He handed her a glass of water. As she lifted herself off the pillow, her head spun.

"Grant, forgive me."

"I'm not God." For a moment, he looked at her; then he picked up his briefcase. She watched him slide across the revolving room to the door and marveled at his balance.

"Do you want me to kill myself?"

With his hand on the doorknob, he glanced over his shoulder. "That would let you off, wouldn't it? You selfish bitch." The door closed and he was gone. She fell into a prickly sleep, dreaming of snakes and ants.

A slam of light woke her. Coumba stood at the french doors, holding back the curtain with one hand, looking out at the sea and the sky. She wore a white headscarf, and the tail of it waved like a flag of surrender as she said, "Du café, Madame?"

"Oui. Et de l'aspirine. Et un Fudgesicle."

A few moments later, Coumba glided into the sunny room and set a silver tray on the bedside table. She sat nimbly on the edge of the bed and watched Thea take the Fudgesicle in her shaking hand.

"You drank last night," she remarked.

"There's nothing like a Senegalese for stating the obvious," Thea said. Then, holding her head, she said, "Pardonne-moi."

"I already forgave you."

"Grant won't forgive me."

"Ah, bon?" Coumba fixed a cup of coffee with hot milk and sugar. Thea waved it away.

"He doesn't love me. Maybe he never did. He's probably sleeping with you, or somebody."

"Ah, bon? The ambassador sleeps with his maid?" Coumba started to lift her robe to show Thea her ruined breasts.

"Stop," said Thea, holding her hand over her aching eyes.

"That old crone said that someone in this house would be unfaithful. You remember."

"Waaw, waaw. You and Bobo — the flirt, what's his name?"

"Elimane."

"He loves you."

"He wants a visa to the United States."

"Yes, that's true."

"Why the hell don't *you* drink the coffee?"

"Moi?" Coumba wrapped her slender black fingers around the ivory handle and took a dainty sip. "It's good. Maybe someday I can go to the United States with you. Not as your maid. I'll just live in your house."

She leaned forward to pick up the crumpled red dress that Thea had tossed to the end of the bed. "Madame is bad," she said, standing up to shake out the dress. In the strong sunlight it burned a hot, flat, sickening red.

"Forgive me."

"I already forgave you." Humming softly, Coumba took the dress to the closet and hung it up; then she went back to the window and looked out. "You know," she said, "sometimes I look at the sky and wonder where it goes. Where do you think the sky ends?"

"I couldn't care less."

"It looks like the sky ends over Gorée Island, but when you go to Gorée Island there is more sky."

"The world is round, not flat. I've explained that to you. I showed you the tennis ball. I told you that was like the world. You pretended to agree with me. God, my head hurts."

"Madame is sick." Coumba shook her head, waving the white flag of her headscarf. "That's a shame." Then she looked back out the window and her face screwed again into a frown. "Do you know," she said, "people are like the sky. You look at them and think that you can see the edge, but when you get close to it, it's not the edge. They just go on and on and you never find out where they end."

"I told you," said Thea hoarsely, "it's a tennis ball." As she rolled over, the sheet wrapped around her legs, tightening as she kicked and squirmed like a monkey in a bag.

When Grant came home she was waiting for him in the corner of the couch. She wore his gray Harvard sweatshirt, and her face was streaked with tears. "Forgive me."

"Don't start. I'm going to get a beer."

Soundlessly, Coumba entered the room and handed him a cold beer. Then she retreated to the alcove just outside the door, where Thea knew she sat and listened to their conversations, following them by the tones.

"I'm sorry, Grant."

He sat down in a chair he never sat in and switched on the TV. When he finished his beer, Coumba appeared with a fresh one, a plate of crackers, and his favorite brie. "Jërë-jëf," he said.

Coumba studied the TV. Deciding that the picture of a white woman cleaning a bathroom was a commercial, she said, "Forgive Madame."

"I was jealous," said Thea. "You'll think this is silly, honey, but we went to this witch —"

"Waaw, waaw," said Coumba, agreeing with the expressions on Thea's face.

"And she said that someone in our house would be unfaithful."

"Naturally that person would be me," said Grant. He took a bite of cracker and cheese, washing it down with a swig of beer. His voice rose. "So naturally, like a damn child, you go out and have this disco boy sew you up a vamp outfit, no payment, *quoi,* so I'll stop being promiscuous. You made a fool of me last night. You selfish, spoiled . . ." He balled his hands into fists.

"Breathe. Grant, just breathe."

"Shut up."

Coumba looked nervously from one to the other and settled on him. "Baal ko," she pleaded. "Grant, forgive Thea."

He stared hard into Thea's face. She moved carefully out of arm's reach, keeping an eye on his fists. She forced herself to think of his baby picture and the one of the grinning boy leaning into the camera; the way tears still caught on his eyelashes when he cried, the way he would hold his arms straight out until she came into them. "It always amazes me that you accuse me of the exact wrongs you are committing yourself," he said. Now his eyes were flat, dark holes with no more soul than the mouth of a gun. "I hate you."

Coumba's mouth opened then, releasing a high, tremulous wail. "Waaagh!" she cried, falling to her knees before Grant's chair, holding her head in her hands as she rocked back and forth. "Waaagh!"

Grant released his fists. Coumba was talking so rapidly in Wolof that it sounded to Thea as if she were speaking in tongues.

"Ndank, ndank, waay," Grant ordered, putting a hand down on the maid's trembling shoulder. He shook her gently. "Slow down," he told her again. Sobbing, she explained to him in Wolof that she was sleeping with Samba and that Grant should beat her, his wicked maid, not his wife. The *seetkat* was right; someone was unfaithful — Coumba, to her husband. "I did not tell you or Madame because then you would send me back to my husband, and I would have to live in a village where there is no running water and nothing good to eat. This is why I let you two fight." She covered her face with her hands.

"Go to bed," said Thea. "I'll make our dinner."

As she spooned the tomato soup into a pan and set it on the stove, Thea chattered nervously to Grant. When she told him about Coumba's theory of the edge of the sky, she was immediately sorry. Laughing hoarsely, he put his arms around her, slowly drawing her tighter against him until she was pressed into his thick chest, where the heat emanating through his cotton shirt, the familiar beat of his heart, his smell, and the gentle flexing of his arms against her back once again made a nest for her body. "How does it feel to have Emily Dickinson for a maid, Madame Ambassador?" He would laugh until Thea laughed too, touch her until she touched him too, and it would begin all over again, until the next time. She put her head on his shoulder. "I'm just an old possum in the sky," he was saying. "Walking to the edge of the sky. Guess I'll fall over. It's Allah's will. Ho hum." He began to dance her across the kitchen floor. "Careful we don't slip over the edge," he said, dipping her back. "Is that God far away or a little bird up close? Guess I'll just wait until it hits me, and then I'll know."

Her body followed his, yielding, as though they were tethered together. There was a smell of something burning. Lifting her head, she glanced over his shoulder to the shadow of two embracing apes moving along the wall. She clung to him; the apes clung together. "Does my girl still love me?" In the instant that he squeezed her, locking her back into his embrace, her mind sprang free. As the shadow slipped off the wall, she planned her escape: the money, the ticket, the taxi, what she would wear on the plane.

Upstairs, in the master bedroom, Coumba removed the dress from Thea's closet and held it against her body. In the light of the moon, it hung on the hanger like the hide of a serpent, blood red, dripping with sequins.

SPIRITUS

When I was twenty-five, I ran away from home. My parents cheered me on. By that time I had lost a series of demeaning jobs and let my boyfriend get away. On brief sojourns to universities, I had squandered money like a queen. When I settled back into the house, I smoked in bed and complained about the food. I drank all of the bourbon then filled the bottles with iced tea. More than once I told my mother she didn't love me, just to watch her cry.

The Peace Corps took me because I have such a nice face. I look like everybody's sister, everybody's best friend from high school. Strangers walk up to me and say, "You look so familiar." When I decided to leave the country, I showed my mug at the Peace Corps recruiting office in Nashville, lied about everything, and before I could make a second impression, I was shipped to Senegal, West Africa.

I arrived in Dakar with seventy pounds of what I thought I needed to survive for two years in the sub-Sahara: an army knife with a tiny magnifying glass that could be used to start fires; a miner's lamp that fitted around my head and shot a thirty-foot beam; the new-smelling Bible inscribed, *To Darren on her twelfth birthday, from Dad;* the complete works of William Faulkner; the slip and high heels my mother insisted upon in case I was invited out somewhere; and an orange.

As I stepped through the turnstile into baggage claim, four or five Africans rushed toward me, hissing like snakes.

"Breathe," I told myself. "Breathe, Darren."

They were as tall as giants and so skinny that their collarbones showed clearly beneath their shirts. Their skins were solid black; some of them were missing a lot of teeth.

"Sss . . . Mademoiselle," one of them called. "Viens avec moi." Another one took my arm and leaned down into my face, hissing, "Madame . . ."

At first I tried to be polite. "Excuse me," I said. "I need to get by here."

Apparently, no one spoke English. When I reached for my blue backpack, spinning slowly out of sight on the conveyer belt, strange hands slapped down and hoisted it over my head. One of the men screamed something about a taxi, and then all hell broke loose.

"Yow waay! Maay yó bbu toubab bi Dakar!"

"Déedéet! Yow! Danga reew waay! Yangiy sàcc business yépp!"

"Américaine? I love you. I spell some Engleesh with you. Yes! We must marry. Viens, viens!"

"Kaay toubab, kaay. Taxi! Viens!"

On the Peace Corps application, I had described myself as fluent in French, a statement that would have surprised the French teachers who had endured my presence in their classrooms. At the moment, I couldn't summon up a single memory of that language except Miss Zelda's lips puckering in her wrinkled face as she demanded, "Où est Sylvie?" then answered herself, "Elle est à la piscine." The seventh-grade class droned back in bored unison, "Where is Sylvie? She's at the swimming pool."

One of the men who didn't have a hold on my pack reached down and took the safari hat off my head, so I had to clutch the hat with one hand while I pulled on the pack with the other. They were all shouting, and when I said, "Leave me alone!" they looked down at me as if I were a talking rabbit. One man laughed and jabbed another in the ribs with his elbows. We were crammed together in such a tight circle that we might as well have been hugging. I was afraid that I would stop breathing, or get stomped. Finally, I jerked the pack to the floor and sat down on it.

The men pressed in even closer around me. One of them bent down and peered at my face beneath the brim of my hat. I decided to ignore him. While the whole bunch stared, I pulled a set of keys from one of the seven pockets in my camping shorts and unlocked one of the ten tiny padlocks my father had attached to the zippers on my pack. Quickly I removed the orange and zipped the pocket and locked it before they could see my other belongings.

I was peeling the orange when a new man pushed through the crowd. He worked his way into the center of our circle and sat down cross-legged, facing me. He smiled. Then he held out his arms. He didn't have any hands. His arms ended at the wrists in smooth black stumps with pink welts. "Na nga def?" he said. "Jox ma orange." The other men found this hilarious. They motioned for me to give my orange to him.

I didn't know where to look. He sat squarely in front of me, holding out what was left of his arms. He kept smiling and nodding his head, saying, "Orange, orange, orange." He was skin and bones.

"Darren, you're panicking," I said aloud. Since no one could understand me, no one realized I was talking to myself. The Africans watched my mouth, as if I were trying to talk to them. In desperation I said some of the little lies my therapist back home called affirmations. "I am a child of God and I deserve to be here," I said to the circle of black faces around me. "I love each moment of my rich, rewarding life," I told the cripple. "All is well."

I was beginning to think I had gotten off in the wrong country when a tall white man pushed through the crowd. He looked like Rasputin, the nineteenth-century courtier, magician, and holy man whose history had been dropped into my head around the time Sylvie went to the *piscine*. He had the same pointed beard, the same mad blue eyes. "Asalaa maalekum!" he said, and the men replied, "Maalekum salaam!" They waved their arms, talking all at once while he murmured replies and watched the orange roll slowly by my feet. He looked from the orange to the cripple, back to the orange, and then at me sitting on my pack like a hen on an egg.

"Hi there," he said. "New in town?"

He was the other Peace Corps volunteer sent to teach English in Senegal, and his name was Ralph. When he had whisked me out of the airport and into a white van, I said, "You look like Rasputin."

"I know," he said. That cut our conversation short. He looked angry, but it might just have been the beard. After several minutes, I cleared my throat and said, "If I were a man, I'd have a goatee."

He didn't hear me. "Speak up," he said.

I said, "Do you mind if I smoke?"

"No, go ahead. Everybody here in hell smokes." I laughed politely and lit a cigarette. The flight had left me so tired I thought I might have forgotten how to sleep. "Yes," he said.

"Marlboro Man has seen to it that the Senegalese will get their fair shot at lung cancer. I wonder who first sat up in the middle of the night and thought, *Hey, I could get starving people addicted to nicotine so they won't be able to buy as much food.*" He jerked his head at me as if I might be the guilty party, then he lit a cigarette. "I don't suppose the almighty United States government told you that you don't have a job." He waited for an answer.

"No, I don't think so."

"The University Cheikh Anta Diop has been on strike for a year now. We are having what is called *une année blanche*, a blank year. Last semester I taught for a total of three days. Sooo . . . some of our leaders put their heads together and decided to bring in another teacher who won't have a job. You don't have a place to live either, by the way. Oh, details, details."

He told me a harrowing story about tanks crashing into the university and soldiers raping and killing students. We were driving along a landscape as flat and sandy as the moon. The highway was lined with gravestones, and speed limit signs were illustrated with a skull and crossbones. When he saw me looking out the window, he said, "Isn't this the most godforsaken place you've ever seen? When I first got here, I thought: *Oh brother, what have I done now?* I almost flew back to the United States the first day. Look around — it's worse in the daylight. Some parts of Senegal are exactly how I imagine hell."

"Where are we going?"

"Stage de formation du Corps de la paix, or Stage for short. The training camp in Thiès. You'll recognize Thiès by the smell — it smells just like shit. God, I hate that town."

I woke up with a jerk. "What town?"

"Thiès. We are going to Stage de formation," he said, slowly, "the Peace Corps training camp in Thiès. Didn't you read your handbook? You'll be there for three months, if you're not in the forty percent of volunteers who are shipped back to the States for bad behavior or medical or psychiatric evacuation. Last week they took one back in a straitjacket."

I imagined myself in a straitjacket. "Your roommate," Rasputin was saying, "will be Lady Jane O'Reilly. She's suffering from post-prom depression." He lapsed into French. His accent was better than Miss Zelda's, or maybe French sounded better on him because he was handsome. The muscles in his arms rolled as he turned the steering wheel.

"That's great," I said to whatever he had said, but Jane worried me. I imagined a bitch in a ruffled prom dress saying, "No, really. I like your hat. Really. It's cute." She would be pretty and shallow and selfish. She would think I was weird. She would whisper about me to the other prom queens who had turned up in the sub-Saharan desert.

At the entrance to Stage de formation, a guard in a yellow stocking cap set his bow and arrow down to drag the wide gate open for us. He and Rasputin called out to each other, "Asalaa maalekum!" "Maalekum salaam!"

By then my eyes stung from lack of sleep, but Rasputin decided to give me a tour of the camp, so I trudged along behind him. Between two rows of thatch-roofed bungalows, floodlights shone through some twisted trees blooming with slick red flowers. A strange bird whistled over the steady hum of mosquitoes. Everyone else in the camp was asleep except for the guard at the gate and a second guard who crept along the fence, moving his flashlight over the pink hydrangeas that bloomed in the shiny barbed wire.

"This is Walt Disney's version of the African village," said Rasputin. "You won't find another one like it in Senegal." In a round, thatch-roofed pavilion he called the disco hut he smoked a cigarette while holding one arm behind his back in a way that looked very French. Drums beat faintly in the distance. "Mon dieu," he sighed. "Don't you expect to see a giant Mickey Mouse floating up there?"

I looked up. All over the sky, stars shone like yellow eyes.

That first night, I stumbled into my room, dropped my bags, and fell across my narrow cot. After noticing that Jane's mosquito net was white lace patterned in roses while mine was a dull army green, I passed out.

All night I had Aralin dreams. I had started taking the malaria prophylaxis back in the States; it gave me dreams as vivid as LSD hallucinations. Some days I took two of the pink horse pills instead of one.

I woke up in the dark, caught in a butterfly net. I was thrashing back and forth, batting at the flying insects around me as I tried to break free, when I heard Jane scream. I froze.

"Oh, God!" she cried. "God, no, no, no!"

At first I thought the butterfly catcher had slapped a net over her, too. Then I thought she was having sex.

"No," she moaned. "God. Help me!" Her voice went deep, then high up to the ceiling, and all around the dark room. It was a beautiful voice. When I realized she was in pain, I ripped my mosquito net trying to get out of bed.

"I'm coming! I'm Darren, your new roommate. Jane? Are you okay?" I slapped the button on the wall, but there was no electricity. She was quiet as I tripped over my boots trying to get my flashlight; then she cried out again. "Shh," I said, fitting the miner's light around my head. "Hush now."

As soon as the beam of my light hit her, she threw her arms up and covered her face. She did look like something caught in a net.

"Jane? You are Jane, aren't you?" When she turned her back to me, her shoulder blades pressed in and out of a thin white cotton tank like wings. Her skin was the color of Breyer's vanilla ice cream and her hair was all red and gold, sliding across her shoulders in a tangle of curls. She drew her knees up to her chest, exposing a small round bottom in a pair of pink cotton panties.

"Turn out the light!" she yelled. "I'm ugly!" She could have sung opera — she was that loud. "Leave me alone!" She tossed my way, with her arms folded over her chest, then flung them up to cover her eyes. Her breasts were high and round; she had plain, square hands.

I had turned my head away to move the beam from her face, and I was beginning to wish she would shut up when she began to breathe jaggedly, making the ribs jump under her tank shirt, and I realized that she was sick.

"You're not ugly," I said. "You're vain."

She sat up. "I beg your pardon?" She raised one eyebrow, the left one, into a perfect arch.

"You're beautiful," I said. "You should know that."

"I'm ugly." She covered her face.

"Are you sick?"

"I'm fine, really. I'm so sorry to have disturbed you. I didn't mean to wake you up. Excuse me." With queenly grace, she emerged from behind the white lace veil, stepped outside the door, and vomited in a long purple arc. Even her puke was beautiful.

Early the next morning the Peace Corps doctor, who introduced himself as Doc, took her away. I wrapped her in a pink silk kimono I found hanging in her armoire, and he carried her in his arms as if she were a baby. Her face was gray and she hung like a rag doll. Once she lifted her head, stared at me with burning eyes, and said, "Leave me alone!"

"I'll only drop by to save your life once in a while. Don't mind me."

"I don't need any help, thank you. I can take care of myself."

"Who the hell would bring a kimono to Africa?"

"Girls," Doc said.

"Is she going to die?"

"I'm hideous," said Jane. As Doc was unfolding her into the back seat, she said, "I'll have the lemon meringue, thank you."

Doc shook his head and got behind the wheel. As he started the car he looked at me through the open window.

"This is what happens when volunteers don't take their Aralin. They get malaria. Look like fun?"

"Is Jane always like this?" I screwed up my face at her, but she was passed out.

"She has a fever, a very high fever," Doc said. "I'm taking her to the hospital in Dakar."

I went back to our room and sat on my cot. The whole room was the size of my walk-in closet back home in Stipple. In the center of the red concrete floor there was a drain. There was one window with a dark green french shutter, and at the other end of the room, a screen door with longer shutters. A fly buzzed around my head.

The door to her armoire was still open. Her clothes were mostly peach and pink; she had a bottle of Oscar de la Renta, a stack of French and Wolof books, and a copy of *Anna Karenina* that looked like it had been left out in the rain and run over twice with a Harley-Davidson. I breathed in the clean flowery smell of her and closed the door. Then I rolled up her lace mosquito net, tucked in her Ralph Lauren sheets, and put one of my Hershey bars on her pillow, for when she came back.

I lay on my cot and stared at the ceiling, then rolled over and stared at the drain. I killed seven mosquitoes. Then I tried to start a fire with my army knife and miner's lamp. Through the screen door, I could hear Americans and Senegalese talking and laughing in French. They all sounded happy. I started imagining what I would say if somebody decided to come and talk to me, what little stories I might tell. I put on some mascara. I thought about making a list of long- and short-term goals, but it was too hot. I considered writing a letter, but suddenly it was hard to remember people from my other life. I began to hate Rasputin for leaving me alone.

Finally, a drum called everybody to lunch. I sauntered up to the disco hut with the other Americans and some Senegalese men, giving my name when asked and asking names that I forgot as soon as I smiled, and I smiled every time anyone looked at me. The other *stagiaires* had all met in Atlanta for stateside training and had bonded like littermates. They rattled off terrible French to each other, and some of them even spoke Wolof. Someone asked me why the Peace Corps had sent me over here by myself. "I was an afterthought," I replied. When everyone laughed, I felt my neck grow hot. All of the Americans were slim and beautiful with shiny hair, straight white teeth, and camping clothes from L. L. Bean. The Senegalese were so strange that I couldn't look at them yet. I kept thinking of the handless man in the airport.

"Didn't you know that you're replacing the English teacher who was killed last week?" A handsome man with a red beard glanced over at me and added, "Oh, I wasn't supposed to tell her. Sorry." He winked.

"Parlez français," said one of the Senegalese men. "Attention à l'immersion française."

Under the pavilion spread with mats, everyone knelt around big dog bowls and dug in with their hands. I hung back. Although no one was paying any particular attention to me, I felt like they would all turn their heads at any minute and burst into laughter. I slipped back in time and felt my mother's hand pressing into the middle of my back. I smelled her lipstick as she said, "Get in there and participate. Project yourself."

The red-bearded man looked up from his bowl. "Kaay lekk, waay," he said, motioning for me to sit down. "Bisimilaay." I knelt down on the other side of the bowl and watched him dip his right hand into the rice, roll a ball, and pop it into his mouth. I stuck my right hand into the warm red sauce and soft rice. In the center of the bowl there were a few carrots and potatoes and a fish head with empty, blackened eye sockets.

"What happens to the eyes?"

"Pardon?"

"Do they take the eyes out of the fish before they cook it, or do they melt?"

"Attends. I will ask the chef."

"Rokhaya!" he called. A tall, beautiful African woman wearing a bright yellow and blue cloth walked over to us in tiny steps and smiled. She held a pot of sauce.

"Na nga def, Oliver?" she said, smiling as she pronounced his name.

"Maa ngi fii."

She looked at me. "Noo tudd?"

"Darren," said Oliver.

"Mu ngi tudd Rokhaya."

Oliver licked his fingers and looked at me. "She gives you her name. Your new name is Rokhaya." Rokhaya smiled. I smiled back. "Ceeb u jen baaxul xa naa?"

"She wants to know if the ceeb u jen is awful," said Oliver. "Rokhaya is one of the cooks."

"I like it." I smiled. Her toenails were painted black, and her bare feet were painted all over with dots and dashes.

"Baax na!" said Oliver. He smacked his lips. "Baax na lool!"

Rokhaya shook her head. "Baaxul. Rokhaya bu ndaw lekkul dara."

"She says the food must be terrible because little Rokhaya is not eating." I dropped my fingers into the bowl and scooped a handful of rice into my mouth.

"Ana bët yi?" asked Oliver, pointing to the charred eye sockets on the fish head. "Where are the eyes?"

"Xamuma! I don't know." Rokhaya covered her mouth with her hand and laughed.

"Ana Jane?"

"Dem na Dakar," said Oliver.

"Lutax?"

He tried a few words, none of which she understood. He put his hand to his throat and rolled his eyes back in his head, letting his tongue hang out of the corner of his mouth.

"Dem na hôpital?" Rokhaya looked horrified.

"Waaw."

"Am na paludisme?"

"Waaw, waaw." Oliver buzzed like a mosquito and poked himself several times in the arm. Rokhaya shook her head. She made a noise with her tongue that sounded like fingers snapping. Oliver tried to make the same noise with his tongue, but it didn't work.

Rasputin strode over to our bowl. "Asalaa maalekum."

"Maalekum salaam."

"Bisimilaay," said Rokhaya. She spooned sauce from her pot into our bowl and padded away on bare feet.

He knelt down between us and put his hand in the bowl.

"Sleep well?"

"Jane has malaria."

"So I hear. She wasn't taking her Aralin, *évidemment.*"

"Is malaria serious?"

"It's the Senegalese flu."

"Effectivement," said Oliver.

"Of course," said Rasputin. "The average life span of the Senegalese is forty years."

"En effet," said Oliver.

"Is Oliver teaching you French?" Rasputin asked.

"I don't know."

"Well, someone needs to get you started. You'll begin your French classes on Monday, but you should know that *stagiaires* are supposed to speak only French or Wolof at all times. I'll take you into Thiès and show you around — from now on, nous sommes dans l'immersion française."

Later I walked beside him down the dusty road to Thiès. Some wiry boys ran along behind us hooting, "Toubab! Toubab!"

"What does that mean?"

"En français, s'il te plaît. Dis, 'Qu'est-ce que ça veut dire?'"

"Qu'est-ce que ça veut dire?"

"Ça veut dire, 'honky,' 'white,' 'stranger.'"

"Toubab, donne-moi cent francs," said one of the boys. He skittered up beside me and held out his dusty palm for money. I pushed my hand in my pocket and felt the two worn bills that Rasputin had lent me for the weekend. The other boy edged in closer. They were so thin. One of the boys wore a shirt torn open over his stark ribs. His eyes were bright. "Toubab!"

Rasputin stopped. "Ana sa yaay?" he demanded.

"Mu nga fa," said the bigger boy, nodding his head to indicate a woman coming through a dusty field with a bucket on her head.

"Ah, bon. Ana sa pàppa?"

"Mu ngi fale," he said more quietly. Again he tilted his head to the field, where a man appeared to be planting something in the dry packed earth.

Rasputin made a point of turning to look at the farmer bent over, working in the sun. Then he looked at the boy. His eyes were hard. He asked the boy if his father was a beggar. The boy stiffened. His brother stepped in closer behind him.

"Non!" they said together. They waited to see what Rasputin would do. He was twice as tall as they were and could have lifted them together with one arm.

"I only thought," he said in French, his voice level and cool, "that beggars must be the sons of beggars." One of the boys balled his hands into fists; there were tears in his eyes. His brother, the smaller one, pulled him away.

"Kaay," he said, as though coaxing a goat. "Ñu ngiy dem." He stood still though, bowlegged, dusty, and defiant, as Rasputin strode on ahead.

I trotted along beside him. We flew by the Senegalese, who took agile, delicate steps, like horses. The men were thin, and I could see the muscles coiling beneath their shining skin. The young women were all curves, and the older women were fat.

Rasputin was lecturing me about African politics. He rattled off names I couldn't pronounce and spewed out long sentences in French. Until I joined the Peace Corps, the only African country I had heard of was Kenya.

"Ah, bon," I said.

"Tu ne m'écoutes pas." He stared down at me, scowling until his eyebrows met.

"Can we speak English for a while?"

"I can. Can you? Aren't you supposed to be an English teacher?"

"Yes, I can, and no, I'm not an English teacher. I've never taught a class in my life."

He stopped short. "Let me get this straight. The Peace Corps has assigned you to a post as professor of English at the University Cheikh Anta Diop, and you have no teaching experience?" He removed his sunglasses.

"I taught the Busy Beavers at the YMCA. But that was some time ago. I was twelve, actually."

"The Busy Beavers?"

"The four- and five-year-olds. Crafts and games. Art. Naps. Nature walks. In college, I majored in religious studies — then I became an atheist."

"Wonderful." He started walking. "This is divine."

"I've read a lot," I added lamely, coming up beside him. "I had a job at a bookstore, but I got fired for reading the books." He smirked. Encouraged, I went on. "I was a Norrell temporary secretary, but they had to let me go because I wouldn't wear pantyhose." We were coming up on some rows of shacks; the Senegalese swirled in and out of them in brilliantly colored robes.

"Continue," said Rasputin. "Who else fired you?"

"I didn't get fired from my last job, exactly." I slapped at a mosquito on my arm and missed. Sweat was running down my neck, and I wanted a Coke but was afraid to ask if they had Cokes in Thiès. "I was working as a cocktail waitress at Moondance, a blues club in Atlanta, but I quit to go to Boulder and see my boyfriend. When I got there, he said he had fallen out of love with me. I went home to Nashville, but my mother wouldn't have me, so I joined the Peace Corps." I looked down at my moccasins, coated with dust.

"Well, well, well. That's quite a success story." He had his sunglasses on again, so I couldn't see his eyes. He stopped at the edge of a row of shacks and breathed in deeply. "Ah, the unforgettable perfume of Thiès — merde."

I took a deep breath.

"Well?" he asked.

"What?"

"Does it smell like shit?"

"Yes."

"This is Thiès. If you ever get lost, just follow your nose." I followed him inside one of the shacks. The floor was dirt and there were no windows. The shelves behind the counter were lined with dusty cans of milk, instant coffee, sugar, cigarettes, and bunches of leaves. I glanced around for a Coke machine before I caught myself.

"Asalaa maalekum."

The man behind the counter said, "Maalekum salaam. Na nga def?"

"Maa ngi fii, alxamdulilaay. Ana waa kër ga?"

"Ñu nga fa, alxamdulilaay."

"Naka liggéey bi tey?"

"Ndank, ndank."

Rasputin smiled and said something else to show off. I turned my back to him and looked at pieces of blue candy in a box behind a piece of rusted wire cage. There were no price tags. Rasputin bought two cigarettes. I thought one might be for me, but he put them both in his shirt pocket.

"Do you want anything?"

"I quit smoking."

"Good." He sighed. "I'm down to two a day now." He looked depressed, then the man behind the counter said something, and they both smiled and shook hands. When Rasputin moved toward the door, I held out my hand to the storekeeper, but he kept his hands by his sides and stared through me as if I were a ghost.

"Ralph."

"What?"

"He won't shake my hand."

"Come on," he said, laughing. "He's a devout Muslim, apparently. Some Muslims consider shaking a woman's hand a sexual act." As we walked back out into the sunlight he patted my shoulder. "Come on, let's get some peanuts."

We were the only white people on the street, and everyone watched us. A man wearing glasses and a hat stopped on the side of the road, lifted his embroidered robe to his hips, and squatted down to defecate. He stared at us as if we were doing something strange. Rasputin waved and went on. He stopped farther down the road, where a beautiful woman sat at a rickety wooden table under a tree. For a moment they talked to each other about me in Wolof.

"She says she gives you her name," said Rasputin. "Seynabou."

"Seynabou," the woman repeated. Rasputin leaned over her, glancing into her cleavage while she showed us the different sizes of peanut bags and named their prices. Rasputin chose a bag. "Cent francs," she said.

"Déedéet. Soixante-cinq."

She clicked her tongue down in her throat and shook her head violently. Then she named a new price. A baby tottered over to her knees, and she bent down to pick him up, letting her robe slide off her shoulder, showing one breast. Her long black braids fell across her face. Rasputin was all eyes. The orange and green swirls spinning around the yellow suns on her robe gave me a headache; I crossed my arms over my chest and turned away.

A man sitting under another tree glanced at us and then did something so stunning that I almost screamed. He put both hands around his right thigh and lifted his leg, which appeared to be boneless, high above his head. Then, as though the leg were a length of black rubber, he slung it around his neck. Balancing his weight on his haunches, he grasped the ankle of the other leg, tipped over to one side, and began to paddle across the dust with one arm, using the leg around his neck like a rudder, to steer. He crawled toward us, sideways, like a crab.

I lit a cigarette. "Ralph," I said, staring at my shoes. "I feel sick." Without meaning to, I flexed my toes, feeling each muscle in my legs, and straightened my back. The cripple kept sliding toward us over the dirt. When he was right at my feet, he caught the edge of the table with both hands and peered over at the peanuts. Then, without saying a word, he selected a bag, put it between his teeth, and began the long journey back to his tree.

"Wait until you see all the shiny black Mercedes driving around Le Palais du Président in Dakar," said Rasputin. In the harsh sunlight I could see the lines on his face.

That night I got drunk alone in my room. Through the screen door, I heard the rustlings of bats in the trees, and the whispers of *stagiaires* who had already paired off as lovers, some of them with the young Senegalese professors. A man murmured, "Il fait chaud ce soir," and a woman laughed and answered in a husky voice, hesitating over each syllable, "Oui. Il fait chaud en Afrique," and this talk of the weather sounded exciting and obscene.

A few days later a station wagon rolled past the gate and Jane stepped out, tanned and smiling. Her teeth looked whiter in the sun, and her hair shimmered the way it had under my miner's light.

"I knew you were only playing sick," said Oliver. "You went to Club Aldiana."

She tossed her hair. "For one afternoon. After I got out of the hospital."

"Malaria. What a ruse! I'm glad you're back."

"Hi there," she said, and I wanted to say something, but suddenly she was surrounded by people.

Late that night, after we had all gotten drunk at a grimy bar called Le Palais, Jane and I lay on our cots and talked through the mosquito nets.

She told me that Club Aldiana was a resort in Mbour that

catered to German tourists. The swimming pool was shaped like a heart. The luncheon buffet offered five kinds of cheeses and twenty desserts. She had brought me a small piece of strudel wrapped in a napkin. She thanked me profusely for the chocolate bar.

She had a small plastic lamp that clipped onto the bedpost, and when she rested her head in her hand, the light that fell on her hair created a shower of red sparkles. The lamplight illuminated the roses laced through her mosquito net, and I told her that she looked like a bride behind a veil.

"Where's your lamp?" she asked.

"I didn't get one."

"You have to request them from Napoleon. I'll get you one tomorrow."

"Who's Napoleon?"

"He's the short guy who runs things around here. He gives us our walk-about money."

"Jane?"

"What?"

"I can't tell black people apart."

"I thought you had a lot of black people in the South. Didn't you grow up with them?"

"I was afraid to look at them. For a long time, I thought that if you touched a black person, you would turn black."

"Well," she said, pushing her hair out of her eyes, "it's going to be hard not to look at black people in Senegal."

"How do you tell them apart?"

"There are a few tricks to it. Actually, all of us had trouble when we first got here." She rolled over on her back, folded her hands behind her head, and stared up at the ceiling through her net. "I look for one distinguishing characteristic, like a piece of jewelry. My professor wears a silver bracelet every day. A lot of

Senegalese men wear those bracelets, but sometimes they're en-
graved with their initials. You have to look closely. Do you have
a French professor yet?"

"I start class on Monday with someone named . . . oh, I forget.
It begins with an *m.*"

"Moustapha. He's easy to spot because he's taller than anyone
else. When he wears those striped pants, he looks like he's walking on stilts. I'll tell you how to recognize him: he wears Adidas
tennis shoes with snakeskin stripes. Look for them. I try not to
look for an identifying characteristic near the face because I
don't feel comfortable staring. Also, you should know that here,
when a woman looks a man directly in the eye, he takes it as a
sexual invitation."

A few days later, when we were lying head to toe on a hammock
watching the laundresses wash our clothes in long cement troughs,
she said, "Before you arrived, we made bets on you. No one
knew if Darren was a boy or a girl. I said that you would be a
girl, and that you would have short brown hair. I knew I was
right. I knew you were going to be my friend; I was waiting for
you." She kicked her foot against the ground and swung the
hammock. Our legs lay side by side. Her toenails, just reaching
my elbow, were painted peach.

"You're cool. You're tough. Everyone likes you." With one
bare arm she shielded her eyes from the sun and turned to smile
at me. I looked ahead, to the laundress's big black arms pumping
up and down, scrubbing my blue jeans.

During lunch Jane would stay under her mosquito net, drinking water with bleach in it, listening to Bach. She was usually up
most of the night, studying index cards of French and Wolof
words by lamplight. Sometimes I woke up and saw her pink lips
moving silently in the shadow while she turned the cards with

her square hands. When it rained, her hair curled into damp ringlets around her face. At night we lay in our nets and talked about men.

◈

I was Moustapha's only French student. We met for six hours a day behind the bungalows in a round cement hut with a grass roof, no windows, and one door. Inside there were two chairs and a chalkboard.

He rarely spoke English, not only because he had been instructed not to do so, but because he disdained any subject in which he did not excel. "Darren," he said, stepping forward like a dancer, "d'où viens-tu aux Etats-Unis? Est-ce que tu as des frères, des soeurs?" I watched the snakeskin stripes on his Adidas tennis shoes. His legs went up and up. His chest and arms were thin but muscled; his neck was long and smooth. He had darling little ears, and his two front teeth were missing.

"Dis-moi, Darren, aux Etats-Unis, est-ce que tu avais un co-pain? Est-ce que tu as jamais eu un mari?" The words dripped from his mouth — slow, thick, sweet. Turning from the waist, he wrote on the blackboard the conjugation of *avoir*, to have. The smoke from his cigarette curled around his cheekbones.

I approached him as though he were a psychiatrist. "Je ne jamais . . ." I began, untangling the verb in my mind as I imagined Jack's thick hairy chest, his blue eyes. I wanted to tell Moustapha how I spent all of my money on a plane ticket to fly out West and see Jack, about the first night there, how he had held me in his arms, with his legs spreading mine, his bearded cheek brushing my face, and said, "I'm not in love with you anymore." I chewed on my finger, trying to find the French words to tell the story, but in the end I could only stammer that I was never not to be married.

He wrote the corrected sentence on the board and continued

asking me questions in French. Did I have a boyfriend now?
Do blacks and whites date each other in the United States? In
Senegal, men often have more than one wife. What did I think of
polygamy?

I made mistakes to prolong his attention. I said that women
should have more than one husband, but men should only have
one wife.

"Ah, bon?" He smiled with his lips closed over his teeth.

"Moustapha is a challenge for you," said Jane. We were sitting
at Le Poisson Bleu under a huge rubber tree whose gnarled roots
rose out of the ground and reached our shoulders.

"Bonsoir, Mesdemoiselles américaines," said a man staggering
toward us. "Je vous joins."

"Non!" I yelled. If you were nice to Senegalese strangers in
bars they asked you to marry them. I threw my leg across the
empty stool at our table so he wouldn't sit down. Smiling, he
pulled up another chair and joined us.

"S'il vous plaît," Jane began earnestly, "nous voudrions avoir
une conversation privée."

"Ah, bon, tu parles bien français." He leaned close to her and
asked if she was married. She told him that she was married, and
that I was her sister. We hadn't seen each other in some time, she
explained, and we would like to be alone.

"Jane! You've started a conversation with him! Now he'll
never leave."

"Ta soeur ne parle pas français."

"I don't want to speak French. I want you to leave. Va-t'en!"
I waved my hand to shoo him away. "Comprends?"

"Bonsoir." He scooted closer to Jane, then sat as if glued to
his stool, glaring at me. Then he studied Jane's breasts.

"We'll ignore him," Jane said. She turned her back to him and faced me with a smile. The tips of her ears were red. "Keep talking. He doesn't understand English."

"Where does this guy get off thinking he can sit at our table?"

"Moustapha," said Jane, smiling hard at me. "Do you think that your attraction to him is based on curiosity, or . . ."

"I'm not in love with him. He's not even handsome."

"He has a certain appeal. He's aloof, and that can be enticing." She tilted her head. "And he's tall."

"He doesn't have any front teeth."

"I just don't want to see you get hurt. Make sure you get out when it stops being an adventure."

Our guest reached for my beer; I snatched it away from him. He laughed, showing a set of pointed yellow teeth.

"I hope he doesn't throw up on the table," said Jane.

"Mademoiselle." He tapped her on the shoulder. "Tu es belle."

"Let's move to another table," I said.

"I hate to be rude."

"Who's being rude?" We stood up, took our drinks, and moved to a table across the courtyard. After a moment in which he seemed completely bewildered, he followed. As soon as he had settled himself next to Jane, another drunk, apparently deciding that I was lonesome, pulled out the chair beside me.

"Bonsoir, Mademoiselle," he said, leering at me. "Ça va?"

Jane and I stood up. They didn't follow us out of the bar, but it was dark on the street and we walked quickly, staying close together and keeping to the center of the dirt road. Splashes of light fell from the open doors of other bars. From them, men called out, "Mesdemoiselles!"

"Sss!"

"Mademoiselle, je t'aime."

As a man's footsteps slapped behind us, Jane reached for my hand. I squeezed it to stop myself from trembling. Without speaking, she squeezed back. We turned a corner.

"Sss," called the man behind us. "Sss, arrêtez-vous!"

"I'm lost," I whispered. "Do you know where we are?"

"Just keep walking. We're almost home."

One night when the electricity had gone out and we were all sitting on our steps with oil lamps, I padded over to Moustapha's door. He sat in a circle of soft light, barely visible except for his tennis shoes, which glowed.

He said, "Bonsoir, Darren." Sweat trickled down my arms, and I smelled the faint steam of Cutter mosquito repellent. I held my French book out like a pass. "Tu étudies?"

"Aide-moi avec les verbes."

"Bon." He slid over on the concrete step to make room for me, and I sat as close to his long, bent legs as I dared. He looked like a praying mantis. "Pourquoi est-ce que tu portes ta jupe comme ça?" He let his hand fall on the knot I tied in my gypsy skirt to hike it up over one thigh. The tips of his fingers grazed my skin.

I coughed to stop the nervous laugh coming out of my throat.

"Eh?" He touched my elbow.

"Because Jane wears her skirt like that."

"Parle français."

"Quoi?"

"Quoi?" he repeated, mimicking my accent. I turned my shoulder slightly away from him, hoping he would put his hand on my back, or even around my waist, to make me face him, but he sat perfectly still behind me. A mosquito buzzed in my ears. Up and down the bungalow, people huddled in the circles of light, talking in husky voices. Even a student droning, "J'habite au Sénégal . . ." to her professor seemed to be whispering from a bed. The bats rustled in the trees. Someone put a Rod Stewart tape on a cassette player and the music sputtered out on a low battery.

On another step, a professor whispered to his *stagiaire*, who also sat with a French book closed on her lap, "Je suis un moustique. Je te pique." Humming like a mosquito, he poked his finger into her arm, then into her bare leg. Insects swarmed around the lamp, and out in the dark, in the thick, hot air, the swallows of people drinking beer were deep, wet kisses; the bat wings flapping against leaves were clothes tearing off our skin.

Another woman strolled by and Moustapha began to talk to her. My head hurt with the effort of trying to compose something interesting to say in French.

When I stood up, he raised his head and lightly wrapped his hand around my ankle. His fingers went all the way around the bone and then some.

"Où vas-tu, toi?"

"Je cherche Jane," I said. He nodded, recognizing my successful deployment of the tricky verb *chercher*, to look for.

"Jane est ton amie," he said. "Jane is your friend." We were an item now, Jane and I. People said our names together: "Where are Darren and Jane?" or "Ask Jane and Darren."

Jane was in the forestry program. Lately, the foresters had been meeting under a large *niim* tree, around a rope and tire swing. They were all supposed to hang the swing together, to learn cooperation.

I was supposed to learn how to cooperate with Rasputin. Every morning for several weeks he had been taking a *taxi brousse* from Dakar to come to Stage. He would knock on my door, hard, and I would come out to sit with him on a bench under the trees and learn how to teach English as a foreign language. He had arranged for me to practice my new teaching skills on a group of high school students in Thiès and, as this day approached, Rasputin grew frantic.

"How is it that you could have a master's degree in English and not be able to spell 'giraffe'?" He crushed my lesson plan in his fist and tossed it in the freshly raked sand. Then he put his hands on his temples as though he had a terrible headache.

"One *f?*"

"No! No, no, no. It begins with a *g*, not a *j!*"

"Maybe I'm dyslexic."

"Spell it." He sighed, picked up the wadded paper at his feet, and unfolded it across his knee. He was wearing an African costume that day: purple batik pants and matching top with gold embroidery around the collar. Around one arm he had tied a leather string of Senegalese charms, called *gris-gris.* He lifted weights at a gym in Dakar. The muscle in his shoulder rose above the string as he lit a cigarette and blew a stream of smoke between us. "The problem," he said, closing his eyes, "is not the spelling." He tapped the wrinkled paper on his lap. "The real problem here, Darren, is the giraffes. When was the last time you spied a giraffe loping across the plains of Senegal?" He looked at me. "Lions and zebras? These kids haven't even been to the zoo in Dakar. You've seen more African wildlife than they ever will. You're not in Senegal, Darren, you're in the *Wild Kingdom.*"

"What do you want me to write about?"

"I don't want you to write about anything. I want you to teach an English lesson, in the present tense, introducing ten new vocabulary words. We've been over this a thousand times. I showed you my lesson plans. I've lent you a stack of *African Nation* and *Jeunes Afrique,* from which you can gather appropriate material relevant to the current social, political, and economic situation in this country. Where are the files I lent you? Have you read about Sopi?"

"A little." His files of clipped, mimeographed newspaper articles were under my cot gathering dust. I lit a cigarette and turned away to watch a blue and gold lizard slither up a tree.

"Sopi is a new, radical political party in Senegal. In Wolof, *sopi* means change. The young men in this party realize that in the present economic and political system, their degrees from the University Cheikh Anta Diop will get them jobs as *taxi brousse* drivers — if they're lucky. No matter what they study or how well they learn, they will never ride in one of those shiny black chauffeured limousines that circle the presidential palace in Dakar like buzzards. These kids eat millet for breakfast, lunch, and dinner. Most of them don't have running water. Their brothers and sisters die of simple, curable illnesses. What the hell happens to all the aid money poured into this country?"

He was sitting up straight now, and the tendons in his neck stood out. "What the hell is the Peace Corps doing but taking jobs away from Senegalese who are perfectly capable of teaching English!" Suddenly, he sank down as though all the air had gone out of him. "Merde," he said.

Silently, I spelled "giraffe" to myself. When Napoleon beat the drum for lunch, I went into my room. Jane was lying under her mosquito net, fanning herself with one of the pink plastic fans the women sold in the *marché*.

"Na nga def?" I said, crawling under my net.

"Maa ngi fii." She hesitated, then said carefully, "Yow. Am nga problem? Lan la?"

"Xamuma."

"Lan la?"

"Muusuma."

"Axkaay!" She put her fan down. "Yow, muus nga!"

I rolled over on my stomach so she couldn't see me smile. This was the longest conversation in Wolof we'd ever mustered between ourselves: "What's the matter? I don't know. What's the matter? I'm not clever. You are too clever!" The word for clever was *cat*.

"Cat!" she said.

"I'm not a cat! Rasputin says I'll embarrass myself tomorrow when I teach this class."

"Does he inspire that kind of confidence in all of his students, or just in you?"

"I don't know what to teach."

"My best teachers taught me what they loved. What do you love?"

The next day it rained. Holding a red umbrella over our heads, Rasputin flagged a taxi at the gate and directed the driver to take us to a brick building with broken windows, Lycée Normal de Ibrahima Amadou Fall. Inside the classroom sat eight students, all dressed in their Sunday best; the boys wore tailored pants with razor-sharp creases and silky shirts unbuttoned to the middle of their hairless chests; the girls wore long, tight skirts sewn from wildly patterned *lagos,* with matching tops that fitted at the waist and puffed out in fancy sleeves. The girls' hair was intricately braided, and they wore high heels, which made them tower above the boys. If Rasputin spoke to one of the girls, she would hide her face until a boy answered for her.

I didn't say a word to anyone until Rasputin, after introducing me in French, motioned for me to come to the front of the room.

"It's all yours," he said. Then, with an evil grin, he went to the back of the room and sat at a desk, folding his hands in front of him and emptying his face of all expression. The students sat as closely together as possible, pencils poised in their hands, and watched me silently. Sweat poured down my back as I edged up to the broad, battered, teacher's desk.

I cleared my throat and then opened my mouth, but no words came out. I tried again.

"My mother is a fish."

"We can't hear you," Rasputin said from the back row.

"My mother is a fish!" I yelled.

The students stared. Rasputin looked pained.

I glanced down at my dress to make sure that everything was buttoned. It was a plain white dress from my favorite clothing store, Around the World, described in the catalog like this:

> On a steamy afternoon in a Malian market, a woman wandered through the stalls in a crisp white dress. Heads turned. She was tall, with tawny skin, emerald eyes, and in the bright sun, her hair was the color of honey. She seemed cool, elegant, and bewilderingly simple. One of the vendors lowered his eyes and offered her a mango. The men thought it was the woman; the women thought it was the dress.

The hem was splattered with mud. Rasputin had sent me back to my room to change my flip-flops, so now I was wearing the high heels my mother had tucked into my suitcase. The three-inch heels had sunk deeply into the mud, and the soft gray Italian leather was now orange. I took a deep breath, licked my teeth in case my lipstick had smeared, and dove into the lesson.

"Repeat after me: My mother is a fish."

"Mymudsafeesh," said the class.

I hesitated, not knowing whether to praise that or not. I looked at Rasputin for direction, but he was watching me as though I were a stranger.

"Good," I said. "That was very good. Now try again."

When I was satisfied with this recital, I explained that they were learning to speak English with a southern accent, which was superior to the northern accent. Although northerners, often called Yankees, pretended to look down on southerners and often called them ignorant, they were, in fact, jealous.

"Southern Americans have more imagination than northern Americans. They are happier and better looking."

The students watched me with liquid eyes. Rasputin put his head in his hands.

"Can you hear me?"

"Yes," said Rasputin.

"Yez!" repeated the class. They began to laugh. "Yez!" cried a boy, and the others followed him. "Yez! Yez!"

"My mothersafeesh!" someone called out.

"Excellent." I went on to say that this sentence, "My mother is a fish," was an entire chapter of a book called *As I Lay Dying,* written by William Faulkner, a southern writer from Mississippi.

"Ten minutes," called Rasputin.

I glanced down at my lesson plan. Gripping a piece of chalk, I hurriedly summed up the novel, which I had reread the night before. I spoke of mothers, death, and fish. The students stared blankly, politely, all sitting perfectly still. Rasputin was no longer looking at me. At three o'clock that morning, I had come up with a statement that seemed so beautiful I thought surely it must have come from someone besides me. When I read it to Jane over breakfast, her eyes glowed with pride. Now, turning the tattered paper in my hand, the lesson plan Rasputin had insisted that I type even though no one else would see it, I trembled. Rain beat steadily on the roof, leaking in a steady stream through one of the broken windows, down the wall, into a puddle on the floor.

I began: "I saw black people for the first time when I was six years old, in the first grade at Orange Street Elementary School. Someone told me that if you touched a black person, you would turn black. I was afraid. I was afraid that if I turned black, my mother wouldn't recognize me when she came to pick me up after school. Where would I go for supper? What would happen to me? But one day I plaited Lanella's hair, and I didn't change color." I paused. My final statement didn't exactly fit in with the rest of the lesson plan, but it was my favorite, and I couldn't resist reading it. "For who can see the shadings of the human heart?"

I looked around the room. The students sat with their blank

tablets, their pencils still, watching me expectantly. They hadn't understood a word. Rasputin stood up.

"Thank you, Miss Parkman," he said, and the students repeated in a chorus, with their eyes shining, their teeth flashing.

"Thank you, Miss Parkman."

After class, Rasputin said, "I'll talk to you later."

The students all shook my hand, but they gathered around Rasputin, who had taught them the previous summer.

"There were supposed to be forty students here," he said to one boy. "Do the Senegalese melt when it rains?" He spoke distinctly, but not slowly. He repeated the words until the boy understood and nodded, laughing.

"Yez. In the rain we must melt, you know. Here in Senegal we are not so much caring for this sweater."

"Weather."

"Yez." He nodded. "Wetter."

"Weather." He smiled encouragingly while the boy strained the muscles in his face trying to form the word. When Rasputin smiled, he looked like a halfway decent guy. The boys pressed in around him, and the girls hung back, smiling shyly until he motioned one of them forward.

"Salimata, has the cat got your tongue?"

She shook her head and covered her mouth with her hand.

"Yez," said a boy, "the cat has took her tongue today! This is too obvious!"

Rasputin flirted with her until another girl, jealous, stepped forward and spoke some English. Then they were all talking.

When the students left and Rasputin and I were standing by the side of the road under the umbrella, looking for a taxi, he turned back into his nasty old self. A beggar had planted himself in front of us and was chanting, "Yàlla baax na, Yàlla baax na . . ." He held out his gnarled hand for money. He wore a brown shirt with one torn sleeve. His eyes were yellow; his cheeks were gaunt, and his hair was a rat's nest.

Rasputin looked into the old man's face and began to shout in French, "If Allah is so good, why doesn't he help you? Where is your God now?" He handed me the umbrella and crossed his arms over his chest, staring the beggar down. I moved the umbrella a little so that the rain hit the back of Rasputin's head.

Without losing a beat, the beggar continued to chant, "Yàlla baax na, Yàlla baax na, God is good."

"Doesn't Allah help those who help themselves? Huh? Why aren't these kids in school today? Does Allah send the rain so that Senegal will remain poor and uneducated, and dependent on foreign aid? What does your Allah think about that?" His face was red, and the muscles in his arms and neck had coiled into knots.

"Yàlla baax na," said the man, holding out his hand. Water dripped from the ragged sleeve onto his bare, muddy feet. "Yàlla baax na."

Not until we had left the beggar and were sitting in the back seat of a rattling taxi did Rasputin mention my lesson.

"Quite a performance you put on in there," he said. "Do you mind if I ask what the hell you were trying to do?"

"I'm sorry."

"Today's lesson plan, if you remember, was to focus on the members of the family, and then, if there was time, on the names of animals."

"I used 'mother' and 'fish.'"

"Cute. Very cute."

"Où allez-vous?" asked the taxi driver.

"Corps de la paix au Stage de formation, s'il vous plaît." Rasputin turned to me and I looked out the window. A wet donkey clomped by with his head down.

"Who is the ambassador to Senegal?" he asked quietly.

"I don't know."

"Can you tell me how many seats are in the House of Representatives?"

I swallowed, trying not to cry.

"Any idea who the president of Senegal is? What is the capital of New Jersey, Darren?" He lowered his voice, thickening it with sarcastic surprise. "How many states are there in the U.S.A., Professor Parkman?"

I slapped him across the face. He jerked back. The driver glanced in the rearview mirror, at the red handprint on Rasputin's white cheek, his blazing blue eyes, and then at me. He stared for several seconds. Then, seeing that we weren't going to do anything else interesting, he looked back at the road in front of him.

That night, when Jane came in from dinner, I was jumping rope in the space between our cots, crying silently. From the door, she watched. "This is just how I cry," I said.

"You could have put an upside-down shoe outside; I wouldn't have bothered you."

"It's okay. It's how I cry. I don't care if you see me."

In Senegal, one shoe placed upside down outside of your hut means that visitors are not welcome. The professors were always chiding us for kicking off our flip-flops and letting them land any which way.

"If there are no shoes on the doorstep, that means that I've gone to Maison du Passage with Oliver, and you and Moustapha are welcome to spend the night here," she said that evening. She sat on the edge of her bed in a pink satin robe, applying makeup while looking into a hand mirror she had bought in the *marché*. Her auburn hair was swept up on top of her head, and when she arched her neck to put mascara on her lower lashes, she was stunning.

"You look beautiful."

She laughed, twisting her lips ironically. "Right." She sucked in her cheeks to apply blush, put on lip gloss, pressed her lips together, then studied her face in the mirror as though she were reading a letter. She scowled. "I'm hideous," she said.

I sighed and fell back on my cot, watching a mosquito try to get out of the net.

"I have face rot. I'm fat. I'm already sick of my clothes."

"Wear mine."

"Really?" She smiled. "Could I wear your white shirt?"

"Sure."

"I'll wash it and iron it."

"The laundresses do that, remember?"

I swung my legs to the floor, pushed the mosquito net over my shoulders, took my white shirt out of the armoire, and handed it to her. She thanked me five or six times, then turned her back to me, slid the robe away from her white, freckled shoulders, and slipped her arms through the sleeves. The room smelled of shampoo, Oscar de la Renta, and mosquito repellent coils. Outside the screen door, footsteps crunched across the sand. A man said, "Tu vas sortir avec moi ce soir," and a woman laughed softly. Somewhere in the distance, drums beat hard and fast.

I opened two beers with my army knife and handed one to Jane.

"Wait," she said. She switched off the light so the room filled with the blue night, and put on my tape of "Brick House." She was wearing her new black sandals and she had let Rokhaya stain her feet in a geometric pattern with henna. On Senegalese skin, the henna came out black, but on white skin, it was red. Most of the design was on the bottoms of her feet, but some tendrils that looked like tiny leaves on silky new branches twined up through her toes. She touched her hair one more time, then she began to sway her hips.

"She's a brick house," I sang off-key, handing her the beer, "she's sexy, sexy."

"To you, buddy." Her cheeks were pink and her eyes shone. She clinked my bottle again, then we both drank, and in the narrow space between our cots, we danced. We spun around faster and faster.

Then Oliver knocked on the door. "Hello," he called. "Are you naked yet?"

We stood still, giggling. Jane's face froze and her voice rose shrilly as she called out, "Don't you dare come in here!" She slipped behind the door to smooth her hair and look in the mirror. I turned the music down.

After they left, I sat on the edge of my cot for an hour, sick with the thought that Moustapha might not come. I changed clothes twice, dressing down each time. I ate some Twinkies that my mother had sent in a care package. I reread a letter. Once, I pressed my face into my pillow and curled up like a baby. When he finally did knock on the door, I pretended not to have noticed the time.

"Oh, hi," I said.

"Bonsoir. Tu me permets d'entrer?"

"Oui." I stood up from my cot as he opened the screen door and stepped over the threshold. His head nearly reached the ceiling. He looked shockingly black. For a moment I was transfixed by the whites of his eyes. The sheer height of his body in my room amazed me; briefly I wondered if he would fit on the cot. He smelled of perfume and wore jeans, a soft black shirt, and, around his neck, a short gold chain.

"Je m'excuse d'être en retard, mais il y avait des difficultés. Alors, tu es prête?" He stood so still, with his hands by his sides, at once awkward and aloof.

"Oui."

"Où est ta camarade de chambre, Jane? Elle est déjà partie?"

"Elle est partie avec Oliver."

"Ah, bon?" He removed a cigarette from his shirt pocket and bent his head to light it with a match. I pushed my hair behind my ears and started toward the door. He caught me lightly by the elbow. "Mais tu es belle ce soir." He brushed one finger across the sleeve of my shirt. It was Jane's shirt — blue silk. "Tu es la princesse du Stage," he said, blowing smoke past my face. "Viens, princesse."

We took a taxi downtown — Moustapha never walked if he had change in his pocket — got drunk, and had an argument that lasted all through the taxi ride home and rose to a climax just outside the gates of Stage.

"Why will you kiss me in a dark alley and not hold my hand on the street!"

"Je te l'ai expliqué. Les hommes et les femmes ne se tiennent pas par les mains en public."

"I am living in a country where a man can step to the side of the road and take a shit, but men and women do not hold hands in public. Great."

"C'est ça." He stood outside the gate — tall, silent, nearly invisible in the dark. I stepped closer to him and reached out my hand, but he wouldn't take it. "Est-ce que tu vas me laisser pour un homme qui te touchera?" He sounded sad at the thought of me leaving him for another man, which seemed strange since I didn't think he liked me, but I was drunk, and it was easy, out in the dark, with him speaking French and the moon up in a pale fingernail, to believe that we were entangled in a passionate romance.

"I'm sick of men in general." I tossed my head.

He hesitated, then said in slow, careful English, "You are not a plant which has to be watered all the time. You don't need to depend on somebody. I don't depend on people." He tapped his chest. "I have a base."

"I have a base, too."

"I know. You have a family in your country. You have a base in America."

"We don't get along, Moustapha." I drew a line in the sand with the toe of my sandal. "My personality is here, and . . ." I walked several feet away and drew another line. "Your personality is over here."

He turned and began walking away from me. He walked slowly, swinging his arms by his sides, as if he had been alone the entire evening. I heard him greet the guardian in Wolof as he passed the gate.

I followed at a distance and then walked faster, but didn't actually run, to catch up with him in front of the bungalow. There were no shoes on the doorstep, so Jane must have gone to the Maison du Passage with Oliver, and I had the room to myself.

"Moustapha." I stood close to him but didn't touch him. "I'm sorry. Je m'excuse." I took a deep breath. "Will you sleep with me?"

We slept in our clothes, with the mosquito net drawn tightly over the cot. Moustapha didn't even remove his tennis shoes. He held me in a grip that hurt my back, and soon he was snoring. I lay against him with my eyes wide open in the dark. As the hours passed my mind spun, caught, and spun again. Every time I lay down with a man, I thought somehow that he was going to save my life.

Sometime in the little hours of the morning, I heard Jane and Oliver at the door.

"Shh," she said, then screamed with laughter.

"Two jelly beans for me, one jelly bean for you," he said. They both howled.

"Shh," she said, and suddenly she threw the screen door open and fell inside. I heard Oliver catch her, heard them kiss. She was laughing too hard to be kissed for long. She was God-awful loud when she was drunk. Apparently, she had forgotten about the shoe code. Beside me, Moustapha stirred awake and breathed quietly into my neck.

"There's somebody, or somebodies, in your bed," said Oliver.

Jane shrieked. Then she said in a stage whisper, "That's not my bed." She appeared astounded. I sighed. "That's Darren. That's Darren and . . . stop that! I mean it!" Then she was laughing again.

With my face pressed against Moustapha's chest, I listened. I thought she might say something about me, since she obviously imagined that I could sleep through this racket, but they were kissing again and seemed to have forgotten all about me. Between our two cots, their clothes rustled to the floor. Oliver tripped over my jump rope and growled, "Shit." Then they were both in her cot.

Oliver was saying, "Do you like this? Or do you like that? Which one do you like better?" Jane made strange low noises in her throat; the range of her voice was amazing. I pressed my hands over Moustapha's ears, but he pushed my hands down his chest, between his legs, and pulled me closer to him. I thought he would be embarrassed, but this was not like holding hands in public. At the sound of his jeans unzipping, the noise in the next bed briefly ceased. I sucked in my breath, trembling all over and trying not to make a sound as Moustapha pulled me under him and spread my legs apart with his knees.

The next morning while I was in the shower, Jane came into the bathroom, tossed her towel over the door, and stepped into the stall next to mine. I looked beneath the green partition at her brown flip-flops, her hennaed feet. She turned her faucet on and for a long time there was no sound but the water splashing over our bodies. She didn't even yelp the way she usually did when the cold water first struck her head. Finally, when I was washing my feet for the second time, she spoke.

"At least your feet are still white," she said. Then we laughed like crazy. I spent that day and Monday in bed, smoking cigarettes and reading Jane's copy of *Anna Karenina*.

On Tuesday morning, Rasputin knocked on my door. When I opened it, he took a step back and said, "Don't hit me."

"I'm sorry."

"It's okay, just don't do it again." He touched his cheek.

"I was mad. I'm sorry."

"You throw a mean left." He grinned. "It might come in handy sometime."

"I feel bad."

"Enough English. Nous commençons encore." He tapped the notebook under his arm and led me back to our bench under the tree. After our lesson, he leaned back and lit a cigarette. "I need to tell you something, and I'm going to say it in English. Last Friday, another volunteer — who I won't name — and I were called into the Peace Corps conference in Dakar to have a meeting about you. The big dogs wanted to evacuate you."

"Did you tell them that I slapped you?"

"Yes, I mentioned it, but that wasn't the focus of my report. I told them that you were upset because you didn't do as well as you expected in your first classroom teaching experience. I also said that I had insulted you. I've thought about what happened, and I think I may have been pushing you too hard. I recommended that you be allowed to stay."

"Thank you."

"You'll make it here, if you can tone it down. Your French has improved dramatically in a relatively short time. You seem to be making friends. You've got guts."

"What else did they say about me?"

"There was some concern about your attitude. The language instructors turn in biweekly reports on their students, and in his last report Moustapha said that although you were bright and willing to learn, you sometimes showed difficulty adjusting to the culture and were often defiant."

"Fuck him."

He blew a smoke ring and crossed one leg over the other. "Did you?"

"What?"

"Did you fuck Moustapha?" He looked me steadily in the eye. Little shocks set off all along my nerves, like firecrackers, then fizzed out, leaving me suddenly tired.

"So who wants to know?" I said, but my voice had lost its fire.

"Moustapha says that you didn't show up for class on Monday morning."

"Did Moustapha tell the committee that I'm good in bed?"

"Darren, I'm going to play big brother for a minute. This scenario between the Senegalese professors and the female *stagiaires* is played out, again and again, at every stage. These guys sit around smoking their cigarettes, listening to their transistors, waiting for the Peace Corps to send them a fresh batch of American girls. It happens over and over; the woman falls for the flowery French, the Disney set of our African village, the exoticness of a black man. Look around you, Darren. Do you realize how difficult it is in this society for a Senegalese man to have sex with a Senegalese woman? Basically, he has to marry her. For two years I haven't been able to score with a Senegalese woman, and I find them very attractive. Their families guard them like watchdogs. You are alone. I hope you're not looking for love. You have no idea what Senegalese men think of women."

"I think it's time for lunch."

"Don't say I didn't warn you." He gathered his papers and stood up.

"Wait," I said. He turned, looking down at me with his wild eyes. "Thank you for standing up for me at the meeting."

"You're quite welcome." We shook hands, hard, and I went back to my room to give Jane all the details.

She listened, wide-eyed, setting her fan down several times. Then she tightened the belt around her kimono and folded her hands behind her head. She said, after staring at the ceiling, "There's only one problem."

"What?"

"What are we going to do with Moustapha's body after we've killed him?"

"We'll get Rokhaya to put it in the ceeb u jen." I chased a mosquito around the inside of my net with a sock while she got up and played my favorite song on the tape player, "Don't Worry, Be Happy."

Later, we danced; slowly at first, between our cots, then out the door and all around the bungalow. We danced in circles, faster and faster under the white sun, until our hair was soaked with sweat and we panted like dogs. Some professors watched us from a doorstep, and I thought I saw Moustapha move between them like a shadow.

He went back to his village for the rest of the week and didn't show up again at Stage until our dance on Saturday night. I showed off for my substitute professors, started jogging, and had long discussions with Jane about being an independent woman, but I missed him. Sometimes I hung around his doorstep. Once his roommate, Bouba, came out smiling, put his hand on my shoulder, and said, "Où es ton petit ami, Moustapha?"

I said I didn't have any *petit ami*.

"Ah, bon?"

On Saturday afternoon, Jane and I went to the *marché* and spent two hours bargaining for cloth. She bought four meters of pale gold *bazin*, and I bought four meters of green *lagos* printed with red moons and blue suns. We were going to use them as bedspreads, but when we were trying on clothes for the party, we decided to tie the cloth around ourselves, toga-style. I wanted to paint lines across my face, to make myself look like an Indian, but Jane said that I was mixing too many different cultures, so I settled for green eye shadow. Jane braided my hair into as many short braids as she could, and I painted my lips passion red and pushed all of our bracelets on my arms. When I was done, she stepped back to look at me.

"How do I look?"

"Ferocious."

"Good."

Jane looked like a goddess. She had draped the *bazin*, which looked like a fine damask tablecloth, over one shoulder and tied it around her waist with a silky gold cord that I had swiped from one of the curtains at Maison du Passage. She wore pearl earrings and a necklace of tiny bleached fish bones. You couldn't tell that she wore any makeup at all unless you stood right in front of her. Her eyes sparkled.

We each drank two beers, split a kola nut to keep us awake, and walked over to the disco hut, which was hung with Japanese lanterns. As soon as we got cups of punch, Oliver swooped down on Jane. I sat under a pink lantern and drank my punch and hers while I watched them dance. Inside the punch there were fleshy seeds soaked in vodka. I sucked one until I felt like smiling.

"Have you seen Moustapha?" asked Jane, slipping away from Oliver.

"No. Have you?"

"He'll turn up."

"If he does, I'll ignore him." I peered through the colored lights, into the dark hole of dancing bodies, but I didn't see him.

"He likes a challenge."

"I'm not in love with him or anything." I tensed as a black man stepped out of the shadows, but it wasn't Moustapha. When Oliver found Jane again, I went back to the punch bowl.

Suddenly I spotted Moustapha. I looked away. Then I looked back. As he walked toward me, he kept his eyes on mine, and I understood why the Senegalese consider it rude for a man and a woman to make direct eye contact. His gaze was more sexual than a kiss. When he reached me, he took another step forward so his thigh was pressing against my hip. He was still staring at me.

"Bonsoir."

"Hi," I said. I wasn't drunk yet, not sick-drunk, but it seemed that if I jumped up in the air, I might float for a minute. I pretended to be very interested in the conversation of a group of people next to us. He smoked his cigarette.

"Mais tu n'es pas gentille," he said softly. "J'avais ta nostalgie et tu fais comme si je ne suis pas là." When I looked at him, my heart raced. He drew the cigarette to his lips, flicked the ash, studied my dress. "Tu veux dancer?" Inside the disco hut, the bodies were pressed tightly together, swaying.

"Non, merci."

"Oui, merci." He took my wrist and led me into the crowd. He tightened one arm around my waist, smoking with his free hand as he pressed his hips into mine. His step was swift and complex, but he seemed to be barely moving; his body was one long ripple of rhythm.

I couldn't get the beat. I felt as though I were trying to ride a wave and I landed, several times, directly on his feet. Once, I thought he called me Cindy.

"Relax," he said, tossing his cigarette as he wrapped the other arm around me. Then I felt each muscle in his body. "Où vas-tu dormir ce soir?"

"Je ne sais pas." The air reeked of alcohol and marijuana, and the pale colored lights from the Japanese lanterns hung all around like small planets.

"J'ai une chambre à la maison des professeurs," he remarked, as if I didn't know that he had a room at the professors' house up the street.

The drinks had kicked in, and suddenly I felt insulted. When I walked away from the dance floor, he followed me outside the circle of light and stepped in front of me to block my path.

"A quelle heure veux-tu y aller?" he asked, as if I had agreed to go.

"Go where?"

"A la maison des professeurs."

"I might go, or I might stay here. Do you want me to go?" We were standing very close now, but not touching, and not looking at each other.

"Tu ne me comprends pas," he said with exaggerated politeness. He condescended to speak English. "I offer you my room at the professors' house because I thought Jane might have another guest tonight, so you would want a place to sleep. That is all." My jaw tightened and I stepped back. "I was planning to come back here to sleep. Do not be disturbed."

"Nothing disturbs me."

"I hope." He walked off to play Senegalese checkers with the guard. For some time I stood where he had left me, with my legs spread to keep my balance. From across the yard I watched their heads bent over the blue and yellow squares of the game board;

their long fingers slid the pieces in deliberate zigzags. Nothing I could do would make Moustapha look at me.

I removed a crumpled joint from behind my ear, lit it, and hacked as the smoke seared my lungs. Then, with my chin held so high that I faced the blazing stars, I stumbled off to find Jane.

She was sitting alone on our doorstep, and when she saw me, she lifted her head and smiled like a little girl.

"I knew you would come," she said. "I knew you would find me."

"You look depressed. How's Oliver? Did y'all have a fight?"

"Oh, no. I just wanted to sit out here in the quiet for a moment." She drew her knees up to her chest and rested her chin in her hands, letting her hair fall in her face.

"Oliver is dancing with that blonde girl who has a tattoo around her eye."

"Marilyn? The second-year volunteer from Touba?"

"The one who walks like a duck. I don't know her name."

"Marilyn," Jane said brightly. She affected a smile of pleasant goodwill, which fit her face like an enormous rubber nose with a mustache. "I admire her for wearing her village family's tattoo. She's a gutsy girl, very smart, and beautiful."

I snorted.

"She had the gall to ask if I'd slept with Oliver."

"Bitch." I pressed the last of the joint out under the heel of my flip-flop. "What did you tell her?"

"I said, 'That's none of your business.'"

"Oliver is a turd."

"I told him that I didn't have any expectations. We're simply friends. That's all." She put on that face again; it was maddening.

"You're great, Jane. You don't know how great you are — you're a thousand Marilyns."

"I am nothing," she said. "I am ugly and stupid. I am nobody and nobody and nobody."

When I put my arm around her, she stiffened, and I thought she was going to cry, or push me away, but suddenly she dropped her head on my shoulder. Her hair was soft and warm and smelled like new grass; it made me think of America.

"Buddy," she said. I wrapped one of her curls around my finger and let it spring free.

Then, from across the courtyard, Moustapha called, "Darren. Viens."

"He's calling you."

"Let him call." We sat perfectly still, as though we were hiding.

"He's coming over here," she whispered. "No, he's not. What's going on?"

"I'm going to the professors' house."

"Be careful."

"I will."

"I mean it, buddy." She sat up straight and pushed her hair out of her eyes to see me better. "Don't do anything with your heart that your head will hate in the morning."

"Darren," he called, making my name sound cool and simple, "viens."

In the professors' house we sat on some foam mats pushed together on the dusty floor, spread with a batik sheet. We each drank a beer and smoked a cigarette. Then we brushed our teeth and stretched out on the mats. Neither of us had said a word since we left Stage. He kissed me — smoothly, mechanically, like I was just some girl, any girl. Then he took hold of my breasts as though they were the handles to a machine, and I bit him.

He tried to knock me off, but I hung on like a dog and sank my teeth deep into his arm. Muscles snaked under his skin, coiling up hard as he slammed his body on top of mine. He squeezed his fingers into my arms. He rammed his knee between my legs. We fought, rolling back and forth, breathing harder and faster, and I came in a flash of ecstatic pain.

Afterward he got up and came back with a glass of water. When he handed it to me, I drank it, even though the Senegalese don't get amoebas so they never bleach their water. He inserted a matchstick into his transistor radio until Baaba Maal crackled through the static, and then he lay back down beside me. He stroked my hair, whispering, "Je t'aime." Then he held me close against his chest and slept while I lay there trying to remember if *je t'aime* means I like you, or I love you.

In the indigo light of early morning, Arabic chants blasted through the loudspeakers of a nearby mosque. Moustapha moaned and covered his ears. He sat up and rubbed his head. Then he looked at me as if he couldn't quite place me.

"They must think God is deaf," I said. "Do you have any beer?"

He felt his arm where I'd bitten him. "Tu es vraiment alcoolique, toi." He left the room, and in a moment he returned with a warm beer and a package of choco biscuits. We split the beer, a cheap Gazelle, and I let him feed me cookies, one at a time, pretending that he was someone else, and I was someone else, and we were in love.

Walking home on the empty road, we swung hands. Dark clouds had gathered in the sky, and the air was hot and thick.

"It is going to rain, and then I will leave you here," he said.

"Do you melt when it rains?"

"I melt like a cube of sugar."

"Then you must be sweet."

"I am sweet, didn't you know? I am a raindrop."

"What will I do when you melt?"

"You will put me in a bucket and carry me home."

"And if I don't have a bucket?"

"You will put me in your mouth."

"Never," I said, but I held tightly to his hand.

In class on Monday morning he told me that I didn't concentrate. I watched the supple black skin stretch over his collarbone as he drew his hands behind his back and looked down at the crumpled homework on my desk.

"I just wanted to kiss you," I said. "At the professors' house . . . I didn't want —"

"Darren, if you speak English, I won't talk to you. Parle français, s'il te plaît." In the hot, dark little hut he paced back and forth in front of my desk. In precise, elegant French, he said, "I know that you know more than you can say. When I listen to your words, I also hear the words you cannot speak. I understand you in the context of your life here, but you must not expect this patience from everyone. If you cannot communicate your knowledge, the students at the university will not listen to you. They will think that you are stupid. They will not attend your classes. You must concentrate, Darren. You must think before you speak. This is not a joke. When I play, I play. When I work, I work. It is foolish to get drunk every day. I get drunk once in a blue moon."

"Pour moi, il y a des lunes rouges."

"Quoi?"

"I said, For me there are red moons."

"Parle français. Je ne te comprends pas."

I put my head on the desk, hoping that he would step closer and touch me, or say something to console me, but he didn't budge from his position in front of the chalkboard.

"Regarde," he said coolly. "You confuse yourself. You confuse work with play, blue with red, and study with love." Through my fingers, I stared at the hard yellow rectangle of sun in the door. A fly buzzed around my head and landed on my neck. "Love," continued Moustapha, "is an art. You have not mastered this art."

"Fine. What is the art of love?"

He paused, so full of himself that I imagined he would leak out of his own ears, but still handsome, or as Jane said, striking. He lit a cigarette. "In the beginning, the two lovers want to look at each other all the time, but they grow tired of looking at each other. After a while, they begin to see things in each other that they do not like. They grow tired of kissing. They grow tired of looking into each other's eyes, of making love. The art of love is not to look at your lover, but to look in the same direction as your lover."

"The Grecian urn has always depressed me."

"Pardon?"

"I don't know how to say 'depressed' in French."

"J'ai le cafard."

"I have the roach" seemed like a depressing way to say "I have the blues." We looked at each other, unkindly, then I gathered my books, rose from my seat, and walked out into the sunlight. I felt a small thrill at leaving class ten minutes early, and without saying *au revoir*.

During sieste, Jane and I discussed my progress with Moustapha.

"In Stipple, if I did meet a black man's stare, to show him that I wasn't afraid, he said something like, 'Baby, can I walk wi' you?' or 'You lookin' fine.' He said it real low, so that it made me shiver, and I would know that he hated me."

"I don't think Moustapha hates you."

"Do you think he'll fall in love with me?"

"I'm not sure if the Senegalese fall in love the way Americans do. I can't tell. You know, the other day Rokhaya told me that she had a boyfriend, back in her village. I asked her if he brought her flowers. I know that was stupid; I haven't seen a single flower outside of Stage, but I wasn't thinking. She laughed. She said, actually, that she had heard that *toubabs* give each other flowers when they're in love, and she wanted to know why. Senegalese men give women food or money or cloth. She said, 'You can't eat flowers.'"

"Stark, very stark." I rolled over and put my face in the pillow. It was too hot to sleep. The sheet stuck to the backs of my legs and the pillow was damp with sweat. We lay there in our nets with no sound around us but the soft paddle of Jane's plastic fan and the hum of the mosquitoes. The life ahead of me seemed long and hard, and here in Senegal, painfully bright. I thought I might be pregnant.

One night when I was sitting under our rubber tree at Le Poisson Bleu, Jane stuck her head through the doorway and grinned. "Buddy!" she called, striding across the courtyard. "I knew you would be here! I knew!" It was her birthday and she was drunk. "Buddy," she said, looking into my face. Her eyes were so bright they could have been two cities. She crossed her arms over her chest and hunched down so that her hair fell over her face.

"Jane, I love you." I watched her intently. I felt as though I had thrown a rock high and far and waited to see if it would crash through a window.

"It's my birthday," she said, brightening. She reached across the empty bottles between us to remove the safari hat from my head and set it on her own. "It's my birthday, and I don't want to do anything but drink and drink and drink. And wear your hat."

In the hat, she was stunning. After three months in Africa, her hair had grown long and ragged, streaked with sun, and her cheekbones were sprinkled with glittering new freckles.

"You can have the hat." I had to swallow though; I really liked my hat.

"Thank you, but I like it better when it's your hat. I like to borrow it." She raised one eyebrow to the bartender, who immediately began pouring a fresh round of beer.

"You're flying high, Jane."

"It's my birthday."

"Then fly as high you want, buddy. I'll be your ground crew."

The bartender brought our drinks. She thanked him from the bottom of her heart, then turned to me with her glass raised. "Let's make a toast." She watched expectantly as I lifted my drink. Then she chanted, "Here's to you, here's to me. Here's to all the men we love. But the men we love don't love us, so fuck the men and here's to us."

Jane had once walked away, offended, from a conversation where someone said "butthole," but she used the word "fuck" beautifully. We clinked our glasses together and drank. The sun fell all around us in a red light, shining through the high, curved roots of our rubber tree. In the glow of the alcohol, sitting with Jane, I was in paradise.

Four hours later, she was sitting at Le Palais with her head in her hands. I leaned down to pick my hat up off the floor where she had let it fall.

"Let's go home," I said. "You don't want to sit at the Palais and look at these walls. This place is only good in the afternoon, when you're riding the first wave of a buzz."

"Buddy," she answered. Then she looked across the room at Oliver. He was leaning over Marilyn, pretending to untangle a string of beads around her neck.

"Are you okay?"

"I'm fine. You can do whatever you like. Please don't feel obligated to sit here with me. Don't stay here on my account."

"You don't look fine. You look miserable."

She touched her hand to her hair, and I sighed.

Oliver came across the bar and stood behind her chair, tall and handsome. Jane acted as if he were a part of the chair.

"I want to put a pole in," he said.

"Put two in," I said.

"Just as a friend." When he sat down beside Jane, she arched her back and smiled insanely.

"I'm fine," she said.

"Talk to me," said Oliver.

"About what?" She lifted her chin and met Oliver's gaze as if she were hearing a petition from a peasant. She looked a hundred times prettier than Marilyn, and absolutely unavailable.

"She wants you," Oliver said sadly to me. "You're her friend. It's a girl thing." He tilted his chair back, took a long drink of beer, and said in a stage voice, "Men — what beasts!"

"Please, don't either of you feel obligated to stay with me," said Jane. "I'm content to sit here by myself and drink." She reminded us that it was her birthday.

"I'm ground crew," I said.

"Oh, I forgot." She had a great smile, even when she was drunk.

Oliver and I talked her into going to a party at Maison du Passage. Outside, when the three of us were walking down the dirt road, he asked if she was planning to spend the night there or go back to Stage.

"I don't want to make any more decisions tonight," she said.

"Good." I stopped to pick my hat up off the road and put it back on her bobbing head. "If you make one, we'll ignore it."

"You're her friend," said Oliver. "When I ask her what's going on between us, she says 'Nothing.'"

Jane spun around to face him, spilling my hat. "So I'm a liar?"

"I didn't say that."

"He didn't say that." I stopped at a gate hidden in some scraggly bushes. "Is this the house? I don't hear a party."

"Well, I think this is the house," Jane said, "but since I'm a liar, I'm probably lying."

"We're here, so let's go in," said Oliver.

"Pony express!" I bent down and grabbed my knees.

"Buddy!" Jane yelled, running up behind me and landing squarely on my back. She was light, but her feet dragged on the ground as I trotted through the gate that Oliver held open. He had my hat in his hand and a dour expression on his face.

Party droppings littered the path to the front door — beer bottles, cigarette butts, a tennis shoe — but the yard was empty and the house was silent except for low strains of Elvis singing "My Happiness."

On the porch, Jane tumbled off my back, flung open the door, and stood there for a solid three seconds, shrieking. Looking around her shoulder, I saw Moustapha, tall and black in the dim room, dancing hip to hip with a redhead.

At Jane's alarm, he stopped dancing, but as we entered the room, he continued to hold his partner's hands, watching us as if we were neighborhood dogs he fondly allowed in his house.

"Asalaa maalekum," said Oliver.

"Maalekum salaam," replied Moustapha and the girl at the same time.

"Na ngeen def?"

"Ñu ngi fii."

"Naka fête bi? Neex na?"

"Baax na."

Oliver and Moustapha and the girl, a second-year volunteer, continued to greet each other in Wolof and ask how was this or that; the answer was always good, good, good.

Jane had disappeared. I could only stare. I stared at Moustapha, I stared at the girl.

She wasn't drop-dead beautiful, and that hurt. She had short hair and wore glasses; at that very moment, my contacts were killing me. She was wearing blue jeans and a T-shirt, tucked in, and was neither fat nor thin. She looked *nice*. This chick — her name was Cindy — would tilt her head and look at me as if she couldn't understand why I was eyeballing her. Evidently, she wasn't even good for a fight.

Moustapha turned to me and had the gall to ask, in French, how I was doing this evening.

"Very pregnant," I wanted to say, but I couldn't remember how to say it in French. Instead, I said, "Come outside. I want to talk to you."

"Demain."

"No, not tomorrow, now!"

"Tu es abrupte," he said in a low voice, looking at me now, only me, as if he wanted to pound my head against the wall.

"If you don't come outside, I will stay here and embarrass you."

"You embarrass yourself," he said.

Oliver quietly left the room and Cindy stepped back, watching me from behind her glasses as if I might suddenly flame up in spontaneous combustion. Moustapha stood with one hand resting casually in the pocket of his pants, ironed with a sharp crease down each long leg. His T-shirt was neatly tucked into his belt, and his hair was combed and patted flat. He wore the same cologne he had worn the first time he took me on a date, and his eyes bore into mine with a fury that thrilled me.

"Now," I ordered.

"D'accord. Je viens." He spoke to Cindy in Pulaar, his native language, and she replied in Pulaar, the smart-ass. Then he followed me out onto the porch, down the path, through the gate, and out into the dark road. Without speaking, we walked to the *naar* shop at the corner, where he bought five Marlboros from a skinny Mauritanian whose brown eyes watched us from beneath the blue scarf wrapped all around his head and covering his nose. We walked back down the road, stopping just outside the gate where we could hear Elvis singing "Blue Suede Shoes." Somewhere in the distance, a child shouted.

Moustapha loomed over me, all squeezed up inside of himself, and tried to stare me down, but I wouldn't go down. I squinted up at the two moons, trying to make them come together.

Then I said, "I hate you."

"I know." His voice was low and familiar, beautiful out there on the empty road.

"I hate your country. I hate Africa." It was too dark to see his face, but when he struck a match to light a cigarette, the flame briefly lit up his hand, his lips, and his high, sharp cheekbones. His eyes turned down, hidden by their curly lashes. He blew a stream of smoke over my shoulder.

"I know," he said.

"Is that ugly girl your girlfriend?"

"She's not ugly."

"She's a dog."

"She is beautiful inside. I like what she has in her head."

I punched him square in the jaw. I remembered to keep my thumbs out of my fist, the way my father had taught me when I boxed with him as a child. "Make a froggie," he'd said, carefully pulling my thumb out so I wouldn't break it.

"I will kill you," Moustapha said quietly. I was on the balls of my feet, swinging another blow, when he hit back. He hit me in the face; and as I fell he caught me by the wrists. He twisted my arms around in his hands, forcing me lower and lower to the ground until I was squatting at his feet. I had begun to scream.

Out of nowhere, a group of children gathered around us in a circle, laughing uproariously. When one of the boys edged closer, darting back and forth as if this were a game of tag, Moustapha yelled, "Ayca!" but he didn't let go of my wrists. Around us the children laughed and shrieked. One of them called out, "Toubab! Toubab! Toubab!" and the others took up the chant.

"You are too small to fight me," Moustapha said. "Really, I will kill you."

Giggling, the children stepped in closer, tightening the circle around us. When I jerked back, trying to free myself from Moustapha's grip, their shrill laughter beat in my ears. When one of them came in close enough to see my tears, he screeched out to the others and they began to jeer.

"Make the children go away."

"You brought them here," said Moustapha. "You have no shame."

Suddenly, he let go of me. He turned his back and walked to the house. I followed at a distance with the children running behind me, taunting, "Toubab!"

The house was quiet. I went into one of the bedrooms and crawled into a hammock. I wanted to cry, loud enough for someone to come and ask me what was wrong, but I was dehydrated from drinking and no tears came out. There was a hole the size of my head in the mosquito net, and as soon as I worked up a dry sob, a mosquito chomped into my ankle or buzzed menacingly around my face.

I got up early, bought some beer at a Lebanese *épicerie*, and dragged my sorry ass back to Stage, where I sat by myself in the disco hut and nursed the first beer. I knew I'd get depressed if I went back to my room and saw my bed neatly made up with the batik spread that had made me feel so African yesterday, in another life. I would see my miner's lamp hanging on the cot post, with my safari hat perched above it, my high heels set in a pair under the bed, and think, *You could have stayed home. You used to have a decent life all your own in this tidy little room. There was a time before you had a black eye.*

So I sat there in the round, empty pavilion in my stupid evening clothes — a blue lagos pajama suit with gold embroidery, completely wrinkled — and watched the sun grow fat through my Vuarnets.

Then Moustapha appeared. He strolled into the disco hut as if he had his breakfast there every morning, sat down nine feet away from me, and opened a box of choco biscuits. He watched me drink and I watched him eat. He dipped two long, elegant fingers into the small cardboard box, fished out a cookie, chewed, and swallowed. Then, without looking at me, he said, "You make me do things I do not want to do. I have never hit a woman before. I am not Moustapha now."

"Just don't fucking call me Cindy," I said. The guard stepped softly along the fence where the bright pink hydrangeas glistened with dew. Beneath his yellow knit cap, his wrinkled face was still. When Moustapha mumbled a greeting to him, he returned it without altering his gait, but he turned his head. In that glance I knew that he had taken it all in: the beer in my hand, the faint edge of bruise showing beneath my sunglasses, the set of our shoulders as we faced each other.

Moustapha selected another cookie and took a delicate bite. He looked smaller in the sun, and less fierce than he had last night. Even with a hangover he sat up straight and held his head high. I was hunched over, shaking and dry-mouthed. He ate his cookies with the supreme serenity of a prince. When he held out his hand, offering me a cookie, I edged forward like a dog.

At lunch, he sat at my bowl. When I burned my mouth on the kaani, he covered his mouth, too, and said, "We are twins. When you feel pain, I feel pain." The next day he left, without saying goodbye, to spend a month in his village.

In the office where Napoleon guarded the old-fashioned black telephone and doled out our walk-about allowances hung a map of Senegal covered with tiny flags. They carried the names of volunteers and were pinned to the regions in which they would be living, in villages, with a village mother and father and heaps of village brothers and sisters.

DARREN was written on a pink flag and stuck in the capital, Dakar. I was supposed to live in a house by myself, but so far no one had found that house. All I knew about Dakar was that one could buy Four Roses bourbon and Frosted Flakes in a regular supermarket, and that a volunteer had gone there one weekend and come back with a broken wrist. Her taxi driver broke it when she refused to give him her purse. Napoleon told me that I could live with Rasputin if he would allow it, but he never offered to share his four-bedroom house on the corniche, and I never asked.

"I'd complain," Jane said. "First they brought you here a month after the rest of us had arrived, then they informed you that the university has been on strike for a year, so you don't even have a job, and now they can't be bothered to get you a house. What are they going to do, just leave you here at Stage, by yourself?" *They* were the staff at the Peace Corps office in Dakar, not any person in particular, but a host of wizards with round green heads and antennae who controlled our destinies, knew secrets, and seemed far away and easy to fool.

"If I made any noise, they might send me home."

She looked grave. For both of us, that was the worst thing that could happen.

Not that home was so bad; Jane lived in a big white house on a green lawn with rich, beautiful parents, strapping, handsome brothers, and a snobby cat.

My own family was showcase material. In the past, I had sometimes put them on display to lure people to me who might have otherwise thought I was a street person. I let people know that we had an intercom and seven telephones, and that my mother was fifty-eight and still not fat. My brothers had zipped from kindergarten through bar exams with straight A's. Our cars smelled new; we had religion; we recycled.

"You're a survivor," Jane said. She must have said that to me one hundred times while we were at Stage, and I began to think of myself differently. Even if I was the biggest mistake God ever made, I had survived.

On the afternoon that Jane left for her village, I tested her on Wolof vocabulary words for the last time. Since no one in her village spoke French, I drilled her in the basics she would need to survive.

"'I'm hungry,'" I said, sitting on the edge of my cot, facing her as she sat on the edge of hers, legs crossed, arms folded over her chest.

"Xiif naa."

"'Give me some bread.'" My body actually hurt from sadness. The pain began in my hands and moved up into my shoulders and all down my back, digging into my gut. There were faint circles under Jane's eyes; her lamp had been on most of the night.

"Wait. I know it . . . Jox ma mburu." I nodded encouragingly as I flipped through the worn index cards.

"'I'm sick,'" I droned. "'I need a doctor. How many brothers and sisters do you have? My name is Jane. What an ugly baby. Thank you.'"

She knew them all, but she made me go through the stack again and again, until Oliver pressed his face against our screen door and said, "The tram is now departing for Okefenokee Swamp. All passengers please watch your step."

Behind him, someone yelled, "Jane! Kaay ñu dem!"

"Maa ngiy ñòw! Waaw, waaw!" I followed her to the white station wagon, carrying her blue Lady Samsonite suitcase. She wore a stiff new green *lagos* dress that stood out around her thin legs; her hair was braided, making her face look rounder and more freckled than usual. When she was seated in the back of the station wagon, she reached out through the open window and we held hands. She had overplucked her eyebrows, making her look both tough and sad.

"I'm sure that they've put the roof on your hut by now," I said.

"I hope so."

"Remember to put bleach in your water, even when you brush your teeth."

"I will. You too."

"Ñu ngiy dem!" called Napoleon. He gripped the steering wheel, shouted out a few more orders to his passengers while "Midnight Train to Georgia" blared from a yellow Sony cassette player, then he spun off. The station wagon went twenty yards before he ground it to a halt. Someone had brought a spider monkey along. It had been sitting peacefully in Oliver's lap, sucking on a Tootsie Pop, until the car lurched forward; then it jumped up and inserted the sucker in Napoleon's ear. Napoleon slammed on the brakes and jumped out of the car. He screamed furiously at his passengers, who were laughing loud enough to drown out the music. The guards ran over and added their shouts to the general din of English, French, Wolof, and monkey. Finally it was agreed that the monkey could ride on the roof. One of the guards tied it up with rope and bound it tightly to a suitcase. Napoleon marched around the car with his arms crossed over his chest and surveyed his prisoners. Then he repositioned himself behind the wheel, and the station wagon careened out the gate. Jane's pale face watched me through the rear window.

I stood in the tire tracks and let the dust settle around me. I couldn't stand to go back to my room and see Jane's naked cot. I didn't know where to go. After a while, Rokhaya saw me and began walking across the yard, wiping her hands on her *pagne*.

She was liquid black in the sun and she moved with a languid grace. When she reached me, she took my hand and said in Wolof, "Jane is gone. Your friend is gone. Darren is sad today." Then she offered to come to Dakar with me and be my maid.

One day a few weeks later, Napoleon knocked three times on my door. "Darren, viens!" he ordered. "C'est moi! Téléphone!" He waited by the door until I came out, then he marched beside me, as though I might try to run away and not take my phone call. He held the door to the office open for me, then ordered me to shut it firmly. The air conditioner blasted over his desk, a small table of battered wood piled with stacks of papers. On the wall behind the desk were framed photographs of various Senegalese and American dignitaries and in each one, if you looked closely, you could see Napoleon in the background, grinning hugely.

"Tu as reçu un appel de Dakar," he announced. He held the receiver in his hand for a minute before he allowed me to take it, and then he stood with his arms crossed over his chest, watching me closely to see if I would use the instrument incorrectly. In fact, I had only used a telephone twice in the three months I had been in Senegal, both times to call my mother, and the cool black plastic receiver felt awkward in my hand. My mother tended to shout into the phone if I was more than twenty miles away, so I automatically held the receiver away from my ear. At first I didn't recognize the voice on the line. It sounded like someone was crying.

"Mets-le plus près de ton visage!" instructed Napoleon. "Qu'est-ce qu'il y a? Tu ne connais pas les téléphones?" He tapped a pencil on his desk.

Pressing the phone against my ear, I turned my back to him and said, "Hello?"

"Darren, this is Ralph."

"Hi, Ralph." It was hard to breathe. My mind began to whirl

with secrets Rasputin might have discovered: the pregnancy, smoking pot, the time I stretched out on the guard's prayer mat and drank a beer, the rock I threw at a taxi . . .

He was crying. "Darren," he sobbed, "I'm calling to tell you that you now have a house in Dakar. You can move into my house any time after noon today. I've cleaned it up. I think you'll find everything you need here: dishes, furniture, some linens. I'm leaving a few books and tapes for you, and you now own a size eleven pair of cowboy boots. There's a can of polish and a rag inside the left boot —" His voice broke.

"Ralph? What happened?" Behind me, Napoleon coughed. "What's the matter?"

"I can't stay in this country." His voice rose. "I woke up this morning, put on my shoes, and went down to the Peace Corps office. I told them to get me on the next flight out of Dakar. They tried to talk me into staying, but I can't live here another minute. I told them I'll take anything — early termination, med-evac, psych-evac. Why am I here?"

Napoleon said he would like to use the phone now; I ignored him. Ralph was crying again. "What can I do for these people that they can't do for themselves? I taught a total of six classes last year." Then he started talking about bombs.

"People are going to kill each other." He sobbed. "I don't want to die out here."

"Ralph, maybe you should just take some time off. I'm going home next month for a vacation. Maybe you should, too. Give yourself time to think."

"No. I'm out of here." He paused. I could hear Napoleon shuffling papers behind me, coughing, tapping his pencil on his desk, shuffling more papers. In a calmer voice, Ralph said, "Darren, I wanted to tell you that I like you."

"Thank you. I like you, too."

"Au revoir." He hung up.

"Bon," said Napoleon when I put the receiver down. "Qu'est-ce qui se passe à Dakar?"

"Ralph part pour les Etats Unis. Il quitte le Corps de la paix."

"Non! Définitivement? Pourquoi?" Napoleon looked genuinely shocked. "Ce n'est pas possible, ça. Il est malade, ou quoi?"

I shrugged, and answered in Wolof, "Xamuma." Napoleon shook his head back and forth, frowning sadly. Then he picked up his pencil, tapped it three times, and pointed out that I now had a house in Dakar.

The next day I piled my possessions among the goats and chickens and boxes tied with string on the roof of a *taxi brousse,* squeezed in with the Senegalese passengers, and went to Dakar. I got the key to my new house, took a pregnancy test, and arranged a round-trip flight to Washington, D.C. Every Peace Corps volunteer was allowed one abortion. I wrote to Jane:

Dear Jane,

I'm going to D.C. to have an abortion. I'll be home in two weeks. I'm fine.

Love,

Darren

When I flew back to Dakar, Jane met me at the airport.

"Are you okay?" she asked, trying to take a suitcase from me while Senegalese men charged in screaming, "Mesdames! My friends! Taxi!"

"I'm great."

"Ayca!" she said politely to a boy trying to wrestle a bag from me. "Are you sure?"

She whipped us into a taxi, and so alarmed the driver with her Wolof that he didn't try to double the fare. When she had finished inquiring about his second and third cousins and all their sheep and goats, she leaned back and turned to me. "I cried when I got your note. Was it bad? Did you call your parents? Are you all right?"

"I didn't call my parents. I stayed at a hotel in Washington. I drank champagne. I don't remember anything."

"Nothing?"

"I bought the most expensive of everything I wanted. I drank Moët & Chandon. Snow fell. I wrote on a bathroom wall in the airport in D.C. I don't remember what. En effet, I had my first blackout."

"A total blackout?"

"It was the happiest time of my life."

"Are you sure you had an abortion?"

"I thought of that, but I checked the papers on the plane. It's done." I laughed, and couldn't stop laughing until she hugged me.

We stopped by my new house, where, as a tribute to Ralph, I put on the cowboy boots. I liked the way my feet slid around in the leather. I couldn't walk in them without stumbling, but I was going to get drunk, so it didn't matter. Then we went to Thiès. A new Stage was in progress, and the *stagiaires* were having a party.

Even after Jane and I got very drunk, the party was uninspiring. Seeing two women come out of our old room was disconcerting to both of us. The professors were hitting on the new *stagiaires,* who all looked pale and plump and whose clothes seemed contrived, even whimsical. When we left to go to a bar, Moustapha invited himself along.

I walked between them down the dark dirt road singing softly, "Nammoon naa la, nammoon naa la. Maa la raw. I missed you, I missed you more."

"How do you say 'third wheel' in French?" asked Jane. Her Wolof was superb now, but her French was not as good as mine.

"La troisième roue," said Moustapha.

"Je suis la troisième roue."

"No, you're not," I said, putting my arm around her.

"Yes, I am."

I wanted to tell her that if she and Moustapha were both drowning at the same time, I would save her first, but she skipped away from me, singing, "Darren, Darren, Darren." I ran after her and caught her hand. We were on a road the Americans had named Bat Lane, and we sang nonsense songs to drown out the rustling and squeaking in the tree limbs over our heads. It was too dark to see Moustapha, who walked delicately behind us.

As we ran, holding hands, I sang, "Enshallah, enshallah, voulez-vous couchez avec moi, enshallah, mais pas toi, I hope, I hope, you want to sleep with me, I hope, I hope, but not you."

"I'll hum till I die!" Jane cried out, swinging me around in a circle.

Behind us, Moustapha asked in a low, dignified voice what we were doing.

"Three's a crowd," said Jane, sad again.

"What's the Senegalese method of birth control?" I asked. "They say 'Enshallah, God willing,' three times, then they close their eyes and say, 'Alxamdulilaay! Praise God!'"

"They have to do it in unison," said Jane, spinning around.

"I've never heard of that," said Moustapha. He glided up beside us. "I think that you are both acting like children."

"Moustapha is a prick," I said in English.

"Qu'est-ce que c'est qu'un prick?"

Jane told him that it was a pencil. "Darren, please hand me my prick," she said.

"If you don't mind, Jane, would you sharpen my prick?"

"The American rests always a child," said Moustapha.

The bar was bright orange. I sat on a bench, curling my legs beneath me, and Moustapha wrapped his hand around the heel of my size eleven cowboy boot and pushed my foot back to the floor. I returned my foot to the bench. He put his hand back on the heel. Jane watched.

"Don't touch my feet," I said, looking straight ahead of me.

"It's been two months since I have drunk a beer," said Moustapha. He glanced at Jane and then at me as he poured beer from a bottle into my glass. He lit my cigarette. I winked at Jane. Once she had said that Moustapha had nice manners.

"You're not saying anything," she said.

"I'm shy."

"Darren isn't shy."

"There are many Darrens."

Suddenly Moustapha said, "Jane, what do you think of Darren's decision to have an abortion?"

We were all silent. The bad side of my face was on his side. My neck was hot. I leaned forward in my seat and put my head in my hands.

Jane leaned forward and looked around his shoulder at me, trying to catch my eye. I looked at the orange wall decorated with masks. My whole body was hot, then cold, and my head hurt. "I was sad," Jane said slowly.

"What do you think about me?" he asked.

She paused. Then she said, "I think that you were both irresponsible." I stared at a grim wooden mask and imagined Jane looking him in the eye. She could be intimidating.

"En principe," he began, "je suis contre l'avortement." He went on to say that I had never asked for his opinion on this matter. I had just told him what I was going to do and flown to the States.

"It's the woman's choice," said Jane.

"I have not cried since I was six years old," said Moustapha, "but I cried after Darren told me that she was going to murder our child."

"It's a difficult decision to make," said Jane, "but since there was no home for the child, it was better to abort it than to turn it out in the world." I considered standing up and walking out the door. The headache had moved from my temples to the back of my neck. Beside me, Moustapha leaned back against the seat and crossed his legs.

"This is not the United States," he reminded us. "In your country, if you want to raise a child, you have to have money for clothes and doctors and a university education . . ." For a moment, I felt a small warm head against my breast. But there had never been a child, only a stomachache. "You see," he continued, "I have given this some consideration. My mother could have raised it in the village."

"Darren?" Jane leaned over his lap to look at me. "What's going on, buddy?"

I stood up and walked out the back door, down a damp passageway into the courtyard. Leaning against the cement wall, I began to cry. In a moment, Jane was standing behind me.

"I'm sorry," she said. "This is none of my business."

"Sure it's your business."

"No, it's not."

"It's your business if you want it to be."

"I had no idea that this was going to happen tonight. I thought that you two had agreed on the abortion." When she stiffened, I knew that Moustapha was in the passageway. He walked silently into the courtyard.

I felt a little bit sorry for him, for being a man and always on the outside of life. When Jane went back into the bar, I held my arms out and said, "Viens. Tiens-moi," but he would not touch me. He would not even take my hand. "I don't care," I said. I walked back through the bar and out into the street, where I stood kicking pieces of paper off the curb while he paid the bill.

I waited another minute, and then I did the thing I do best: I ran. I sprinted across the street, down Bat Lane, past Stage where the Chinese lanterns glowed around the disco hut, and down a dark road where I had never been before. As the air cut through my lungs, I imagined that I was running through glass. With each stride I tried to beat out even the possibility of sorrow. I wanted to rip my lungs out, blow up my heart, go mad. Then I tripped and fell in a mud puddle.

When I sat up, I decided to face the fact, once and for all, that nobody loved me. This made me cry. I was covered in sweat and slime and one of my earrings was gone. After a while, when I got tired of sitting in the road, I trudged back to camp to see what I could stir up.

A TIME TO THROW STONES

The storekeeper could not pronounce Darren's name so he decided to call her Fatou, after his mother. His name was Karamba; he was a small, quick man with serious eyes and a sweet smile. The neighborhood of Fann Hock revolved around his *épicerie,* a wooden shack roofed with sheets of rusted tin and lit by a single bulb that hung from a stripped wire.

Karamba stocked his shelves with sugar, salt, Nescafé, and gunpowder tea, which he sold in portions as small as a teaspoon, as well as canned milk, soda, beer, and gin. He sold Gold Coast and Marlboro cigarettes singly or by the pack. Every day he dispensed two cigarettes to Alioune, the local idiot. Once, in moment of fancy, Karamba had bought several boxes of Belle Lady hair coloring — blonde — and these sat on the top shelf gathering dust until Darren moved into the house around the corner. She was the only white person for miles, and Karamba took it upon himself to teach her Wolof.

This morning, when she strode in swinging her keys on a chain looped through a can of Mace, he smiled broadly and said, "Bonjour, Fatou. Na nga def?"

"Maa ngi fii," she replied. "I am here."

"Where is the Peace Corps?"

"It's there," she said, and sighed, looking around the store. She stared for some time at the Belle Lady boxes.

"Where is your work?"

"I have no work. The university is on strike."

"Ndeysaan!" he exclaimed. "Mother is sad!" He assumed an expression of sorrow which he held for two seconds and then let pass like a cloud, revealing another smile. "And where is your American friend, Jane? Does she like living in her Senegalese village?"

Jane hated her village so much that she refused to stay there more than two nights in a row. "She likes her village, bu baax," Darren said. "A lot!"

"Where is your husband?" Karamba smiled slyly.

"I have no husband."

"Why not?"

"Amoon naa ay jëkkër, waaye rendi naa leen yépp," said Darren. She drew her finger across her throat like a knife. This was the most complex thing she knew how to say in Wolof, and she was very proud of it.

Karamba gasped. "You slit your husbands' throats? All of them? Laa illaa illalla!" Holding his throat with his hand, he stepped away from the edge of the counter, as though she might whip out a machete.

Then he asked, "Will you slit the throat of the man who comes to your house to teach you French?" Darren examined a roll of toilet paper on the shelf, pretending not to understand his Wolof.

"What's his name?" asked Karamba. "Is it Moustapha? Will you kill Moustapha?"

He lifted the can of Mace she dropped on the counter in order to take the toilet paper from the shelf. He turned it gingerly in his hands. "What's this?" He rested one finger lightly on the trigger, and the keys on the chain tinkled softly against each other. He held the can under one of his armpits as though it were deodorant.

"C'est le gaz," said Darren. She pushed some hair behind one ear, then nervously chewed on her finger.

"Ah, bon." Karamba stopped smiling. He turned the Mace over in his hands, even more carefully than before. "C'est sérieux, ça."

A moment passed in awkward silence. Outside, children shouted in rapture. Their voices were high, thin, and, Darren thought, crazy. She was terrified of the African children. When they stared at her with those clear, unblinking eyes, the nostalgia of childhood evaporated; she remembered how savage it had been. Now they were screaming, "Alioune! Alioune!" Darren tried to ask, nonchalantly, for a bottle of gin, but her voice shook, and when the madman came to the door, she froze.

He stood in the doorway with his head grazing the ceiling and his shoulders blocking out the sunlight. He was barefoot, and his feet, like his hands, were enormous. It was a hundred degrees today, but he wore a wool sweater that seemed to be unraveling around him of its own initiative. The sleeves, both too short for his long arms, were of different lengths. On his head was a wool knit cap topped with a fuzzy pink ball. Darren thought it might be a child's cap; it was much too small for him. In the dim light of the single bulb, he looked almost like a ghost. "Fatou," he said, using the voice of a woman. "Na nga def, Fatou?" She stepped back, closer to the counter, and tried to yawn as though she were bored, but he had seen her shudder. "Fatou," he repeated, raising his shrill voice. "Fatou, Fatou, Fatou. Na nga def,

Fatou?" He was looking directly at her now, with flat, silvery eyes. They were like mirrors. "Ça va?" he asked. "Fatou. Ça va, toi?"

Without looking up from the tea he was measuring into small plastic bags, Karamba told him to go away.

"Lan la?" Alioune took a step forward, which put him half-way across the room and let in a flood of sunshine. He pointed a long skinny finger at the Mace lying on the counter and said, "C'est le gaz." Then he looked at Darren. "Toubab," he said. "Toubab, donne-moi une cigarette," he demanded.

"Get out of here," said Karamba, as though he were talking to a stray dog. "Go on, now! Get!"

"I'm talking to the *toubab*." Alioune planted himself directly in front of Darren and folded his arms across his chest. "Toubab. Donne-moi une cigarette."

"Go outside," said Karamba. He looked suddenly tired. The fool stepped into the doorway and leaned against the frame with one foot in the store and one foot on the ground outside. "Out!" yelled Karamba.

"I am outside." Alioune tapped one bare foot on the packed earth to prove it.

"All the way out!"

Alioune glared at Darren.

"Léegi," warned Karamba. When the storekeeper came around the end of the counter and started toward the fool with a raised hand, Alioune moseyed out into the street, acting as if he had lingered in the store out of sheer politeness. He disappeared around the edge of the building.

Karamba shook his head and sighed. "He's an idiot," he said in French. He tapped his finger against his temple and told her the Wolof word, *dof.*

She nodded.

"En anglais?"

"Madman," she said.

"Mod mon." He smiled. "Mod mon. Modmon. Ah, bon?"

Darren had forgotten to bring a bag to the store, so she carried the toilet paper, cigarettes, and bottle of gin wrapped in newspaper under her arm, leaving one hand free for the Mace. She thought Alioune might be lying in wait for her around the corner, but she saw him playing contentedly with some children across the street. He sat on his haunches, his long arms draped around his knees, looking quite serious as a boy spun a wire hoop with a stick in a circle around him. The wire flashed in silver threads, spinning around him so fast that he looked like an animal crouched in a cage. When he saw Darren, his expression changed. "Go home to your lover, *toubab!*" he yelled. "Go home!" The children chimed after him, "*Toubab, toubab.*" The only one who didn't join in the chant was a small boy named Yaya who lived in the apartment beneath Darren. He was her landlord's son, one of twelve children, and by far her favorite. While the other children threw small sticks and gravel at her back, screaming "toubab," Yaya stood with his hands in his pockets, like a tiny old man, squinting solemnly in the harsh white sun until she had made it safely to her door.

In the kitchen, Darren fixed herself a gin and tonic. When she had drunk three of these, she put Billie Holiday on the cassette player she had convinced the Peace Corps she needed to teach her English classes and, humming along to "My Man," laced up her rollerblades. The blue plastic wheels were still shiny; she had bought the skates only two weeks ago, when she flew to Washington to abort Moustapha's child. "He's not much on looks, he's no hero out of books," she sang as she rolled across the black and white tiles of the living room with her arms outstretched, her knees bent. "But I love him, yes I love him." She skated through the open bubble-glass french doors into what she called her suite; a tiny bedroom with a narrow window and a water-stained ceiling, and a room with a cheap battered desk that led out to a wide balcony shaded by the waxy green leaves of a mango tree. On the balcony, she tried a 360. Feeling light-headed, she rolled out of the suite and down a long, grimy hall that opened into two dusty bedrooms, around the kitchen, where she paused to top off her drink with more gin, and into a master bedroom that had a large, blue-tiled bathroom with broken plumbing. Holding on to the sink with both hands, she looked at her flushed face in the cracked mirror and said, "Are you the kind of woman who always has to have a man?" Jane had asked her this when they were roommates at the Peace Corps training camp in Thiès, making Darren hate her for a full hour. Now she lifted her chin and cut her eyes.

"No," she said. She tried again, turning her head to the side. "No, Jane, I am not that kind of woman." She pushed her lank brown hair behind her ears so that her cheekbones showed. "No, I'm not the kind of woman who always needs a man." She smiled ever so slightly. "Are you?" She reached her finger into the waistband of her gym shorts, touched the lips of her vagina, and brought her finger up to the light to see if she was bleeding. A nurse at the abortion clinic had told her she was supposed to bleed some but not a lot. Darren decided she was bleeding the right amount and skated to her bedroom to get ready for her French lesson.

When she had removed her skates and changed into a dress, she flopped across the narrow bed and reread the letter Moustapha had sent her the week before. It was written on pale blue stationery and reeked of perfume. "Appropriate for the flowery language," she had told Jane. He had given her the *pagne* she was lying on; he was displeased when he saw that she was using the cloth as a bedspread. She assured him that she would take the material to a tailor to be made into a dress as soon as she could decide on the style. The cloth was hot pink patterned with electric blue and yellow wheels, each as large as a tire. "It's wax," he had informed her. "The wax is more expensive." Now she smoothed it under one hand as she sniffed the letter and read:

Ma chérie, ma petite amie, ma copine, comment puis-je te décrire comment mon coeur s'envole vers toi? Tous les soirs je pleure de joyeux larmes, tellement notre amour est grand. C'est toi, la femme qui a changé ma vie.

Using a French/English dictionary to translate, she had scribbled in the margin:

My dear, my sweetheart, my girlfriend, how can I describe to you how my heart takes flight toward you? Every night I cry joyful tears, so great is our love. You are the woman who has changed my life.

The letter went on like that for three pages. It was a mystery to Darren how anyone could put so much effort into being insincere. He was even talking of marrying her. Or had that been before the abortion? He told her flat out that he considered her a murderess. Then, for a few weeks, he attached himself to her like Velcro. This was not his style. When he was her French professor at the Peace Corps training camp, she had stalked him, and more than once he had tried to shake her. "What is your attraction to him?" Jane would ask, and they would spend the entire evening talking about it over drinks, but Darren never dared say what she really thought: It was exciting to hate. It was sexy.

She looked at the clock; he was late again. She put the letter away, fixed herself another drink in the kitchen, and carried it to the narrow balcony that opened off the living room.

Moustapha arrived in a taxi. A sun screen with a life-size

portrait of Marilyn Monroe covered the back window and he seemed to emerge from beneath her: a tall, thin, blue-black man. Darren waved. He smiled with his lips together; he was missing his two front teeth. Once or twice she had seen him smile with his mouth open. She had almost liked him then, snaggle-toothed and bashful.

She ran across the living room and down the steep white stairs to let him in, but he took her by the elbow and led her outside. "Our lesson today," he said in French, "is how to walk like an African woman. The Americans are always running, as if they were being chased." Darren tramped ahead of him, looking coyly over her shoulder, but he kept his expression neutral. She swung her arms and kicked up dust with the heels of her sandals. Behind her, he said levelly, "A great man once said, 'It is a fine art to saunter.'" Moustapha had been a philosophy student at the university for a few weeks before the professors went on strike, and he liked to pontificate. He studded his conversation with deep silences and was a master of the poker face. Every time he told her, "A great man once said," Darren knew that in his mind, this great man was Moustapha himself.

Playing a game with herself in which she was a wild, beautiful girl he meant to capture and force into sexual slavery, she tried to fall into step beside him. However, she had no rhythm, and she found it impossible to walk that slowly without coming to a complete stop. She felt like a teenager in a ballroom dancing class. She was watching her large, dusty feet when she noticed the lizard. It walked between them, lifting its legs in delicate arcs. She looked from the lizard to Moustapha and back to the lizard. The reptile had an eye on each side of its head; it looked neither to the right nor to the left, but stepped along with graceful purpose, ahead of its magnificent tail. "Regarde," she said. At that moment, Moustapha and the lizard both turned their heads.

Their throats undulated. "I feel so white," she said. "I feel like a snowball."

"What is a snowball?"

"Snow. You know what snow is, don't you?"

"La neige," he said, flaring his nostrils in contempt. "I've heard of it."

"A snowball is a ball made of snow. It gets bigger as it rolls through the snow, but it melts in the sun."

"Then you will melt in Africa." He touched her lightly on the wrist.

In the house, she made lunch while he sat at the rickety kitchen table, conjugating verbs. "S'écouler," he called out when she turned on the faucet.

"M'écoule." She dumped the tomatoes in the sink. "Tu m'écoules."

"Non! You speak French like a ballsnow."

"Snowball?"

"You do not know how to move your tongue because you do not know how to move your body. Begin with body. Enleve ta robe."

"Moustapha, I'm trying to cook."

"This is not sex. This is grace. Remove your dress." He folded his hands on the table and watched while she unzipped the back of her soft cotton dress, pushed it off her shoulders, and stepped out of it with her back to him. "Le soutien-gorge," he said brusquely, and she unfastened her bra, dropping it on top of the dress. She knelt down to remove her panties, hiding them in front of her body and hurriedly stuffing them inside of the dress before he could see that they were stained with blood. She felt his eyes on her and was sure that he was criticizing the faint ripples in the backs of her thighs, the thickness of her waist. A former lover had told her that men were not nearly as critical of women's bodies as women suspected, but Darren never believed him. "Bon," Moustapha said. "Fais la cuisine."

Darren took three steps to the refrigerator and opened the door. In the cold air, her nipples froze into hard points. "Glisser," he said in a low voice. "Je glisse. Tu glisses . . ."

"Il glisse," she said faintly. "He slides. She slides. It slides." When she looked over her shoulder, she saw only the clothes on his body: white Adidas tennis shoes with snakeskin stripes, new blue jeans, pink shirt. His favorite color was pink. Behind his head, tacked to the wall, was her map of Senegal. She thought how different its shape looked to her now than it had when she arrived in the country six months earlier.

She cracked an egg against the rim of a glass bowl.

"Doucement!" he said as her body began to convulse with sobs.

The next day, when Karamba was wrapping her bottle of gin in newspaper, Alioune came into the store. He pretended not to notice her but she read his mind as though he were her lover or her worst enemy. Sometimes she was afraid that he knew what she was going to think before she did. There had been other times in her life when she attracted crazy people, but no one had ever come after her with Alioune's intensity.

He spoke in English. "I am going to come to your house and drink gin with you. I am going to fuck you." In a split second he stepped behind her, ran his finger down her spine, and walked out of the store.

"Va-t'en!" yelled Karamba, truly angry. Senegalese rarely touched white people. Once a boy on the street had grabbed her arm with both hands, and people gathered all around to chide him. "Tu la salis!" one woman cried indignantly. She lifted Darren's white shirt sleeve to show that the boy had left a dirty handprint.

I am like Alioune, Darren thought that evening as she prepared for her date with Moustapha; *I don't follow the rules.* In her own way, she was a perfectionist. By seven forty-five she had put fresh, ironed sheets on the bed, lit candles in all the windows, and arranged the coffee table with a bowl of ice, a tray of sliced limes, a bottle of gin, a bottle of tonic, and the two glasses that almost matched. She put the Billie Holiday tape in the player, fixed herself a drink, and went out on the balcony to wait for him. She was wearing her white dress and had curled her hair and put on makeup.

At the end of the tape she combed some of the curls out so she wouldn't look as though she was trying to impress him. Halfway through a Rod Stewart tape she decided to change back into jeans. When she stood up on the balcony with an empty glass in her hand, she heard a whistle.

It was Alioune. He stood beneath her balcony, smoking a cigarette. Except for the ridiculous pink hat, he looked fairly normal. Then he screeched in his old woman's voice, "Bonsoir, Mademoiselle. Comment allez-vous, Mademoiselle?" He dug his fingers into his cap and tugged, imitating the way she had tried to comb out her curls. "Est-ce que je suis belle?" he whined. He began to dance up and down as if the street burned his feet. "Aw, aw!" he squealed, waving away the amorous advances of an imaginary beau. "Je ne t'aime pas!"

"Dof!" screamed Darren. A neighbor walking along the street looked up at the candlelit house and Darren stormed inside. Later, she walked around the corner to a barroom the size of a bathroom. It was run by two pretty whores who sold silty red wine in Coke bottles. Darren stayed for hours, filling the juke box with C.F.A. coins, buying rounds, speaking French to the men who sidled up to light her cigarettes. When she stood up to leave, one of the prostitutes took her hand and walked her all the way to her house.

"Those men are bad," she said. "They will follow you and rob you." The woman, who was dressed in a black negligée, tightened a dirty pink shawl around her shoulders as she looked up with awe at the big white house, clean in the moonlight. "Tu habites ici?" she asked. "Seule?"

"Yes," said Darren, leaning in the doorway. "I live here alone."

"Tu es riche alors!"

Darren shrugged. She had grown up in a wealthy family and always managed to attract money, but somehow the gloss of elegance never showed up on her. Her mother pushed for more makeup; her father smoothed her hair as he talked to her about table manners, but no matter what she wore or where she went, the creatures her parents called subhumans recognized Darren as one of their own.

Moustapha turned up late the next night. When Darren didn't answer the door, he called up to her balcony from the street, "Darren, c'est moi, viens." She had no intention of letting him in, but she looked in a mirror all the same. There was still some curl left in her hair from last night; when she twisted the brown locks in her fingers, they rose reluctantly back to life. His voice floated up softly into the empty house, disturbing twenty-four hours of silence. "Darren, est-ce que tu es là?" She went out on the balcony to tell him to leave.

He stood under a streetlamp, smoking a cigarette. His white silk jacket glowed while the rest of him receded into a tall shadow. Although she knew that he slept in a bed with other men and often didn't have money for bus fare, Moustapha looked rich. He always used a lighter, never a match. He never drank from bottles, but always asked for a glass. He walked, sat, and stood as though he was constantly being photographed. No, there was really nothing to him, but she grabbed a jacket and went down the stairs to be with him, and her heart pounded with excitement.

They took a taxi downtown to the Bar Américain, where she followed him up the spiral staircase that led to a single table on the roof. After the waiter brought their drinks, they were alone in the treetops, very close to the moon. The sky was an eerie color, almost green, and Darren became intensely conscious that she was in Africa. With a pen, Moustapha wrote his name on the back of her hand. "Regarde," he said. "I can write on you, but you cannot write on me." She pressed the pen across the back of his long, smooth hand, but the ink was invisible on his black skin.

"Were you with another woman last night?" she asked. Her fingers twisted nervously on her lap under the table, but she smiled at him as if she were making polite conversation. When he did not answer immediately, she began to hate him. She hated the way he leaned back in his chair, the way he held his chin, the way his eyebrows fell into delicate curves under his high forehead.

"You mustn't think that every man you love will love you back," he said.

"I'm seeing someone else," she lied. "An American."

"That is your choice."

"Were you with another woman?" She lost her patience and slammed her fist on the table as her eyes filled with tears. The wilder she got, the more serene he became.

"A great man once said, 'Let the guiltless person throw the first stone.'"

She turned her face to the moon. It seemed so close that she imagined she could reach her arms over her head, clasp her hands around it as if it were a smooth, yellow stone, and hurl it across the table at Moustapha.

When she stood up and began to walk away, she had no intention of leaving him. Certain tricks were universal and she couldn't have said where she first learned them, or why she was unable to replace them with honest action. As she stepped across the tiled roof she was aware of the moonlight falling around her, the drape of her hair, and the turn of her hips. This worked so well that she could have left him and still felt like a sex goddess for several hours, but of course he was following her. He wasn't in a hurry. His sneakers barely whispered on the tile. She sashayed; he glided. She loved the effect of her cigarette smoke spiraling up as she turned down and around the spiral stairs. He caught her there. He kissed her so that she felt his teeth. With one arm he held her against his hard penis until she became dizzy and excited and didn't care if she died.

When they sat again at the round table under the moon he let her grow cold and hate him again before he reached his hand across the table, as casually as if he were reaching for his drink, and unbuttoned the top three buttons of her dress. As he closed his eyes, he slid his fingers over her bare breast, drawing smaller and tighter circles that finally spiraled into her erect nipple. The bats broke noisily through the trees, flying so low she could see their bellies.

The next morning, when it was still dark outside, he got out of bed and stepped into his pants. In the light from the streetlamp, his belt buckle flashed between his long black fingers.

"Don't go," she said.

"C'est dommage, ma chérie, mais je dois partir." He spoke matter-of-factly and kept his eyes away from hers.

"Tu prends du café?"

"Non, merci." He bent down to look in the mirror that hung on her wall and patted his hair with the palm of his hand until the kinky curls lay flat and smooth. He remarked that he needed a haircut.

"Come tomorrow," she said.

"Non, ce n'est pas possible." When he sat down on the bed she thought that perhaps he was going to make love to her again, and she wet the inside of her mouth with her tongue, but he was only putting on his socks and shoes.

As he rose, he lit a cigarette. Blowing smoke on her, he said, "There was blood on the sheets."

Inwardly she cringed. In college she had gone to bed with a cocaine dealer who woke her up pointing a pistol at her head when he discovered that she had menstruated on his white satin sheets. It wasn't the gun that made her cry; it was the shame. Moustapha had told her that it was a sin for a Muslim man to fornicate with a woman who was having her period. It made him unclean, he said, and she told him he could take a damn bath, but still she was ashamed. She had never liked the way women smelled.

"Je n'ai pas mes régles," she said. She couldn't think of a way to explain that she was supposed to bleed for a while after the abortion. The thought was completely irrational, but she was afraid he would think somehow that they were still killing the baby. She began a halting explanation in French, but he interrupted her to say he had an appointment and would return a week from tomorrow. Too much sex destroys a man's will, he reminded her. He didn't smile.

"Ciao," she said.

In English, he said, "See ya later, alligator."

After he left, she stayed in bed until Alioune had one of his fits. They seemed to come most often during the first hours of light.

When Jane was staying with her, they woke each other up to watch Alioune lose his mind in public. They joked that he had gotten up on the wrong side of the bed. There was nothing funny about the spectacle when Darren had to witness it alone, however. This morning, the experience was harrowing.

She lay in her bed staring wide-eyed at the cracked ceiling while she listened to him roar somewhere outside her walls. He bellowed, he shrieked, he got down on his knees and barked like a dog. Only once before had she heard the human voice in such a hollow, lonesome caterwaul. In the abortion clinic in Washington, Darren's cot had been placed next to a thin wall through which she could hear a machine's buzz and then a woman's crying. Soon that patient was rolled into the recovery room, and in five minutes the machine hummed again. Darren, who had not paid the extra hundred dollars for anesthesia, had forced herself to float up to a corner of the ceiling, from which she could observe the room.

It was interesting how each woman made a different sound, and how they all came together in a chorus. Darren clung to the copper pipes running along the ceiling, afraid to come crashing down on the other women. Then a big dark woman with long black hair was rolled into the room, wailing so loudly Darren couldn't hear the others anymore. She pulled her own hair and screamed in Spanish. Then she began to wail. The sound was tremendous. It hollowed out Darren's stomach and made her tongue itch. On and on the woman wailed. Sometimes she stopped to catch her breath, or yell something in Spanish, but before long that sound came out of her again. The noise hurt so much that Darren fell from the ceiling back onto her cot, where she started to scream for her paper bag of clothes.

Now, as she lay on her bed listening to Alioune, she wondered if she was going insane. In the back of her mind she had always wanted to be a little mad, but she didn't like this. She was afraid that without actually meaning to, she might go outside and touch Alioune, to feel the place on him that made him bellow. It occurred to her that he might kill her.

He was still hollering when she forced herself to get out of bed, put on a bathrobe, and get a beer. The beer calmed her down. Finding her cigarettes, she stepped out onto the balcony and looked over the railing. The street was empty, but she heard him coming.

He turned a corner and stormed up her street, cursing the world. He stopped beneath her balcony and screamed, "Damay kat sa ndey! I'm going to fuck your mother!" to everyone and no one. With a hand the size of a cast iron skillet, he slapped at the air. For a while, he fought an invisible enemy, then he just stood in the middle of the street and howled.

No one else in the neighborhood was paying him any attention. A beggar stood by the wall with his bowl, gumming some breakfast; a vendor sailed by with a carton of eight dozen eggs on his head; and a maid, after smirking once, went on sweeping the doorstep. Suddenly a group of children swarmed around the corner, from the same direction the madman had come.

"Alioune!" they shrieked. "Alioune! Alioune!" Once or twice he lunged toward them, but they only squealed and knocked back into each other. After a moment, he stopped trying to chase them off. When he began to wail again, he moved along down the street, turning sometimes, waving his arms now and then, and the children followed him in a pack, as if he were the pied piper of Senegal.

Luckily, Jane turned up that afternoon. She stood on the street yelling at the top of her lungs, "Hey, buddy! Open up! It's me!" She banged on the door until every single neighbor looked out his window.

"Announce yourself next time," said Darren, flinging open the door, but she pulled Jane inside and hugged her tight. She

squeezed her arms all the way around Jane's ragged green backpack, ran her hands through the long, tangled curls. Then she
stepped back and watched her smile. Jane was so beautiful that
Darren thought she spilled some beauty when she moved. They
began to laugh and talk at once, so thrilled to speak English that
they shouted.

"How's the village?"

"Village-bi sucks bu-baax a-baax. I hate my village mother! I
hate my village brother! The dog eats out of my food bowl. I'm
so glad to be in Dakar. How are you?"

"Weird. Okay, I guess."

"Sure?" Jane bit her lip and looked hard into Darren's face.

"Yep. I'll fix some cocktails, and we can talk on the balcony."

"Wonderful. Do you mind if I take a shower? There's a hole
in the bucket I use for my bucket bath. I'm sure my brother,
Zuro, put it there. He's a real wit."

When Jane reached the top of the stairs, she shouted just to
hear her voice echo.

"You live in a mansion!"

"It's full of ghosts!" She ran into the middle of the living room
and spun around on one toe. "Dancing ghosts." Darren put on
an Ike and Tina Turner tape and danced while Jane took a bath.
The house seemed to come to life. Sun poured in the windows,
which were just squares cut out of the plaster, covered with iron
bars. Even the dust motes were lovely; they fell softly through
air that was sweetened now with the smell of Jane's shampoo.
The vinyl chair that held her backpack now had a purpose. Most
important of all, the night no longer lay like a curse waiting for
the end of the day; Jane was here.

News that Darren had a visitor spread through the neighborhood. For the rest of the afternoon people meandered along the
street, staring up at the balcony until they were satisfied that they
had witnessed with their own eyes the two white girls sitting

together drinking beer. After Jane's hair had dried, eliminating the interesting sideshow of wet *toubab* hair, the crowd thinned out.

"Ah," said Jane, picking up her beer, "civilization."

At that moment Alioune stopped in front of the house toting a sack of garbage he had decided to sell as a chicken. "Jëndal ganaar gi!" he called up to them. "Buy a chicken!"

"Oh God," said Darren.

"Is it the madman?" Jane leaned forward to get a better look at him.

"He was working through some of his feelings of aggression this morning."

"I'm glad he hasn't started repressing anything."

"Nope. He's wide open." Darren crossed her legs and lit a cigarette.

"Mille francs," called Alioune.

"No, thank you," Jane called back in Wolof. "We already have a chicken."

"You speak Wolof," he said. "You're white, but you speak Wolof? Why can't Fatou speak Wolof? Na nga def, Fatou?"

"That's me."

"I'm not white," Jane called out, leaning back in her chair. "What makes you think I'm white? I'm black. I'm Senegalese." He walked around until he stood directly beneath Darren's legs, which she had propped up on the railing.

"You're upside-down," he said. "I'm black. You're white."

Then Jane hung her head over the balcony and said, "No, you're upside-down, look."

"Get rid of him," said Darren.

"Fatou!" he hissed. The pink pompon on his cap bobbed as he craned his neck back to see her.

"He's bananas," said Jane. She giggled, then leaned back over the railing and called out, "Yaa ngiy dem." She said it as though he had been insisting all along that he must go, while she politely detained him. To Darren's amazement, he left.

"He's only funny when you come over," Darren said. "He must have a crush on you."

"No, you're the one he loves. I can tell."

"Say I sell him to you."

"Say," said Jane, imitating Darren's Southern accent as she handed her a fresh beer.

"Make nice."

"Say, how are things with Moustapha?"

"Fine."

"Really?" Jane raised one eyebrow, a trick she used when she wanted to make someone tell the truth.

"We have a date tomorrow night."

"I'll leave before then."

"No, please don't. Please stay."

The next night, showered and wearing clean clothes, they sat on the balcony with their drinks and watched taxis go by. When one of the cabs stopped, they both leaned forward, but the man who got out went to the house across the street. The cabs kept inching around the corner, swinging Marilyn Monroes under the streetlamp.

"I hate that Marilyn Monroe screen," said Jane. "No wonder they think all American women are prostitutes."

"It's very white." Darren took a long drink and said, "I don't think he's going to show up."

"She actually looks dumpy in that bikini."

"Do you think he's going to show up, Jane?"

"If he doesn't, it's his loss."

"Right." Darren finished off her drink and stood up to fix another. "I don't like him anyway."

"I never knew what you saw in him."

"I liked his teeth," said Darren. "Cheers."

Several hours later, when she was fixing herself a nightcap in the kitchen, Darren saw red pushpins zigzagging across the map of Senegal. "Jane?" she called, stirring the drink with her finger. "Jane, did you do something weird to my map?"

Jane appeared in her pink silk kimono. It had not fared well in the village and was almost gray now.

"I did." She lifted her chin. There was no arguing with her when she did that.

"What the hell is it?"

"Those are Moustapha's girlfriends, Darren. I marked each town and village where he has a Peace Corps volunteer mistress."

Darren sipped her drink, staring at the jagged red line the pins cut across the country. Then she pulled the pin out of Dakar.

"I'm sorry," said Jane. "I didn't know how to tell you."

"He was just a fling."

"But he was your fling." She put her arms around her, rocking her back and forth. "You're tough," she said, and the words echoed in the dark, silent kitchen.

The next day, Darren came back from the *épicerie* with a box of Belle Lady hair coloring. Jane studied the perky blonde on the package, then looked over at Darren. "Are you sure you want this? I'd try something more . . . subtle first."

"White on white. Just like Marilyn Monroe. Bleach me."

When it was all over, Darren sat in front of the mirror, staring.

"You look very, um, very white," said Jane.

"I need red lipstick. I need fake lashes. I need to look like something unreal."

"May I ask why?"

"Because I'm too approachable."

"You've just been approached by the wrong people."

"This will change." Darren opened her mouth and outlined her lips with a red pencil.

After Jane returned to her village, Darren sat down with a French dictionary and wrote Moustapha a letter that began, "You're fired. You are no longer my French teacher or my lover." She told him that he bored her, which wasn't true, but she knew it would hurt him. She added a few nasty remarks about his performance in bed, then put the letter in an envelope, sealed it, and carried it downstairs. Since the post office was on strike, she would ask her landlord's son Yaya to deliver the letter in person.

When Darren knocked, a woman holding a toddler opened the door. "Bonjour," said Darren, delivering a red-lipstick smile. "Je cherche Yaya." From the time the door was open, the toddler had not taken its eyes off Darren. Now it screamed. The scream seemed far too large for the child, it seemed to come from somewhere miles deep, and the force of it nearly strangled the baby, who choked and screamed again, struggling for the strength to scream harder. The woman found this hilarious.

"Yaya!" she yelled into the foyer behind her. "Yaya, kaay fii!"

The boy appeared. Darren noticed that his head had recently been shaved; the skin was as smooth and brown as milk chocolate. The woman said something to him and he giggled, looking at the baby, who was still screaming.

"The baby thinks you're dead," Yaya told Darren, grinning. "She thinks you're a ghost because you're so white."

When Darren left Yaya, the baby was still crying somewhere back in the house. Yaya understood that he was not to mention the letter to anyone, and that he would report back to her as soon as he had delivered it to Moustapha. When he took the letter in his hand, his face assumed the punitive expression children wear when they try to imitate adults. Although the address was several miles away from Fann Hock, he set off at a sprint.

In a short time he knocked at Darren's door.

"Fait accompli," he said, brushing his hands together.

"Entre." She went upstairs for some coins, expecting him to follow her, but he hung back, keeping the door open with one foot.

"I am not a ghost," she said firmly. "Shut the door and come upstairs if you want to be paid."

"Bon," he said in the faintest whisper, and trotted up the stairs. She put him on the couch in the living room, gave him a cold Coke, and went to look for her purse in the bedroom. When she returned, he was staring at the Mace attached to the chain of keys lying on the coffee table. "C'est le gaz?" he asked her in a hushed voice. She pressed a bill into his palm; this gave him courage. "Do you kill people?" he asked.

"No," she said, sitting down beside him. "Aren't you going to drink your Coke?" He reached for the soft drink as if she might take it away from him. Then he nodded toward the Mace and asked, "What does it do?"

"It makes people cry," Darren said. She drew tears down her face with her fingers and repeated slowly, "Tears, tears, tears."

"Tears," he said in English, sticking out his bottom lip. He was a bright, beautiful child, and it struck her suddenly that he had probably never even owned a toy in his life.

"I want to give you a present. What would you like?"

He waited so long to answer that she was afraid he was going to ask for a bicycle. He looked ecstatic with hope. "Toilet paper," he said finally. "Pink." He beamed at her. When he saw the incredulity in her face, he cast his eyes down. "Karamba sells it at the *épicerie*," he mumbled. When she took him down to the store to buy his toilet paper, Karamba covered his eyes with his hand, as though her blonde hair had blinded him.

"You are so beautiful now," he said. "I will take you for my second wife."

That evening, Darren skated through the house, looking at her white hair in the mirrors, talking to herself. When she rolled out onto the balcony, Alioune, who had been leaning against the wall across the street, looked up. For a second he seemed to freeze. Then he shielded his face with his arms and began to scream.

The next day, at noon, an hour in Senegal as oppressively silent as midnight, when the shops are padlocked, the houses are shuttered, and the streets are still, Yaya passed by Darren in his crown. It was constructed from bits of wire and pasteboard, and three hundred feet of pink toilet paper. The crown bloomed in pink petals of joy, swept around in figure-eights of grace, and whirled up into the heavens where it exploded in triumph that unfurled along the child's back and arms in banners of glory. Under this fantastic headpiece, there was nothing left of the plain Yaya from Fann Hock except two dusty feet in flip-flops. Darren waved to him, but his head was lost in its pink cloud, and he sauntered across his new kingdom without seeing her.

When he disappeared into an alley, she felt that she had lost sight of hope. The sun bore down on her head, and her cotton pants clung to her thighs as she waded through the air. The street was empty now except for three men sitting cross-legged on the side of the road; they seemed familiar, but the sun was so strong she could not make out their features. She stopped, and was squinting with her hand over her glasses, when Alioune sprang.

Crossing the street in two bounds, he screamed, "Diable! Devil!" His face twisted into a knot and he let out a roar, flecking her face with foam. "I'll kill you!" he screamed. Her heart slammed against her chest as he swung his open hand and knocked her to the ground with a thud.

Immediately she scrambled to her feet, then crouched back down and froze. He had picked up a stone. It was a smooth, gray stone the size of her head. He raised it with both hands, thumbs touching. A second began and crept along. A soft breeze stirred her hair against her skull, and she wanted so badly to cover her head with her arms, but she could not move. She could not take her eyes away from the stone. Her temples pounded, and she felt a profound love for her life, for all life. As he lifted the stone back over his head, the muscles roped in his arms, pressing veins against his thick skin. He aimed. She began to keen. It was an animal sound: gut-scraping, piercing, and obscene. She could not hear it.

Then there were two men grabbing Alioune's arms and the stone dropped to the ground. She watched it roll past her feet and thought for a moment that she was seeing her own head. One of the men bent down and picked up her glasses. When he had fitted them on her face, she saw that it was Karamba. "Are you hurt?" he asked. She shook her head. "Go home," he said, helping her to her feet. "Return to your house."

Across the street, Alioune dawdled, as if he could not decide what to do next. When Karamba screamed at him in Wolof, he scowled and slunk away. It was difficult for Darren to walk. She had to lift each foot and watch it land in the dust in front of her. When she unlocked the door to her house, she realized that she had been clutching the Mace in her hand the whole time.

Moustapha came that night. She opened the door for him and said, "I hate you. Do you think a woman can't hate you? Why do you think you can come to my house?" She spilled the glass of wine she was holding; it ran down her blouse in an ugly red line and he frowned.

"You're drunk," he said, stepping into the foyer. He was wearing a silky black shirt, open at the throat, and in his hand he held a snakeskin folder. She knew that her letter was in the folder.

"You're too tall," she said, slurring her words as she backed up the stairs to make herself bigger than him. She held the Mace up, hoping that he would see it and leave before she sprayed him. He didn't seem to notice it; he was looking at her hair.

"Darren," he began. "Cette situation est très compliquée."

"Shut up." The tendons in his neck thickened into cords, and he gave her a hard stare. Then he removed the letter from his folder and began to read her words aloud to her, correcting the French as he went along. She could smell his cheap after-shave. "Cry," she said. "Sob. Weep. Let the tears fall," and she sprayed the gas into his face.

He jumped forward and caught her wrist, then fell back, pulling them both out the door and onto the street. Tears poured from his eyes, wetting his neck, even dropping onto her head. Steadily, he turned her wrist as though he were twisting a lid from a jar. When she began to scream, the neighbors peered through the square windows in their metal doors, but no one came outside.

Then something crackled above them, in the branches of a mango tree, and a small black creature landed on Moustapha's back. "Don't hurt my friend!" Yaya yelled, beating his fists around Moustapha's head. "Leave her alone!" Moustapha, with gas tears still pouring down his cheeks, let go of Darren to pull the child off his back. Yaya hit the ground, then jumped up and stood between Darren and Moustapha, trembling all over as he held his skinny arms out in a shield. Moustapha spat and staggered down the street.

When he was out of sight, doors began to open. "Lan la?" the landlady asked. Someone called out, "Ana góor gi?" Someone else yelled, "Fatou, kaay fii," but Darren didn't answer. She hugged Yaya and told him that he was brave. Then she went back inside her house.

When the first light of morning came into the room, she left the house. The sky was dark blue, and the light bulb in the *épicerie* shone like a star.

"Na nga def?" asked Karamba.

"I'm here," she said, touching the lump on her head. "Where are you?"

"I'm here." He handed her a cigarette from his shirt pocket and leaned across the counter to light it for her, cupping his hand around the flame.

"I need some things," she told him. "Du Nescafé, du lait, du sucre, des crayons, des cahiers, des Marlboros . . ."

"You're going on a trip, Fatou?" He stacked the notebooks on the counter. "Du chocolat?" She nodded.

When she felt Alioune's presence, she turned around to face him. He stood in the doorway, barefoot, wearing the same patched pants, sweater, and knit cap. She let him stare. She waited for him to carry out whatever idea might spark in the frayed wiring of his brain. He stared at her with those flat eyes like mirrors. Then, slowly, he drew two long, black fingers down his hollow cheeks, in the imitation of tears.

THE GUIDE

At the gate of the Grand Hotel du Mali, a brothel that served as an inn for the rare tourist in Oulaba, Darren paid her first guide. The child had only carried her pack up the short path from the road, and his dark eyes grew round as he took the one hundred C.F.A. coin into his fist. Immediately, the other boys attacked him, pawing for the money. "White lady!" one of the children shouted in French. "We all led you here. We are all your guides, and you must pay all of us!"

Darren shook her head, banged the gate shut behind her, and went down a dark corridor. Behind one of the closed doors, a whore wailed. Her voice rose and fell in a siren, now laughing, now crying, following Darren down and around the halls to the courtyard, where the sound of the television drowned it out. The black and white set perched precariously on a stack of crates, balanced by two rabbit ears. Beneath the screen, Malians sat on mats, mesmerized by a fuzzy, French-dubbed episode of *Dallas*. They barely turned their heads as the small, pale American wearing a man's felt hat crossed the courtyard to the bar.

"Bonsoir, Madame," she said to the stout woman leaning in the doorway. "Je m'appelle Darren." She asked for a room for the night.

The hotelkeeper looked her over. She uncrossed her arms to wipe her hands on the faded *pagne* wrapped around her hips and reaching to her ankles. Then she folded her arms back over her chest and returned her gaze to the white woman in bed with her lover on the TV screen. The gold ring in the hotelkeeper's nose glinted in the dim light.

From a shadowy corner of the room, a boy stepped forward. "Bonsoir, Madame Darren," he said. He bowed low, like a magician on stage, and said in French, "Please excuse my mother, for she doesn't speak the languages of the first world. My name is Jaraffe, and I am at your disposal." He offered a brilliant smile. "American, I presume? Americans are my favorite people. How do you find Mali? If you care to see our cliffs tomorrow, I am pleased to be your guide. You are tired. Perhaps you would like a beer? I suggest the imported beer. Normally, of course, one can't find such luxuries in Oulaba, but this is your lucky day." He lifted his thin shoulders in an elegant shrug.

She wanted to laugh at him, but she was stunned by his beauty. He was slender, with skin the color of honey and silky black curls that fell into damp ringlets at the nape of his neck. His nose was precise and delicate; his lips curved salaciously, blood red against small, even white teeth. A new T-shirt, several sizes too large, slid off one shoulder, baring the bones of his chest. As she studied him, he kept his head demurely bowed, hiding his eyes beneath their lashes, but suddenly he raised his head and stared back. He had the yellow eyes of a cat.

"How old are you, Jaraffe?"

"Me? Well, I am thirteen. No, not thirteen. Did I say thirteen?" He affected a bemused chuckle and stretched himself up taller. "I am fourteen, actually. Almost fifteen."

"I'll have the imported beer," she said, sure that he would return with a flat, warm Gazelle, or something worse, and a long explanation. She sat down at a low, rusty table and rested her head in her hands. In a few moments he reappeared with an icy bottle of Heineken. She held her hand out before she caught herself.

Then she narrowed her eyes in the expression of jaded wariness that she adopted in her dealings with Africans. The expression was fake. She was alone and, more or less, lost. In a leather pouch hanging from her neck and tucked inside her khaki pants she had five hundred dollars — more money than the average African earned in a year. If she had to, she would pay an outrageous price for the cold beer, and the child knew this. "How much?" she asked.

"For you, my friend, seven hundred C.F.A."

"Six hundred."

He shrugged, handed her the bottle, and returned to his stool in the corner. After a weary sigh, he removed a crumpled cigarette from his shirt pocket and approached her again. "Do you have a light, Darren?" When she shook her head, he found some matches in his pocket, smiled apologetically, and, lighting his cigarette, sat down beside her.

The game began. Darren considered telling him that she had not invited him to sit with her, but she was too tired to get tangled in the absurd exchange that would inevitably follow such an announcement, and after all, Jaraffe was only a boy.

Three days ago she had set out from Senegal on an odyssey to Timbuktu, and since then she had not had a moment's respite from African men who considered any young white woman traveling alone to be public property. Her furious protests were as delightful to these men as if they came from the mouth of an unbranded cow wandering in their fields. In the first hour of the train ride from Dakar to Bamako, a note was pressed into her hand:

> Hello my American frend. I find you is so very nice for me. So yes you pleese me. I love you. Now we will be together. Nice.

For the next twenty hours, no matter where she sat on the train, the man wedged himself in beside her, smiling indulgently at her rejections. He did not consider himself rude.

Now, having gained a seat at her table, Jaraffe sailed into the relationship. "Are you married, if you don't mind my asking?" Smoke curled softly out of his lips and hung in the moist air between them. He wasn't inhaling.

"Yes," she lied.

"Your husband is an oil tycoon, perhaps? Or a doctor? It's none of my business. I myself will be a surgeon. When I have saved enough money, I am going to America to study medicine. Now, when I am not in school, I work as a guide. I give most of the pay to my mother, of course, but I save what I can for my journey to America. Perhaps you and your husband would like me to take you to the cliffs tomorrow? We can go and return in a single day, if you like."

"I wasn't . . . my husband and I weren't planning to go to the cliffs."

With a wave of his hand, he dismissed this detail. "I know the cliffs. The other boys will ask to be your guide, but, unfortunately, they are all liars and thieves."

"Thanks for the information, but we don't need a guide."

He smiled at her bad French and continued. "For you, my friend, I will only charge fifteen thousand C.F.A. a day, or fifty American dollars if you like. You see, I must go to the cliffs tomorrow anyway, because I have a secret mission there. My father is a *marabout* — a magician, if you will. He can turn rocks into coins, he can make your enemies run when they see you coming down the path, and he can make it rain." He paused, watching her with his yellow eyes. "He can make the dead rise again."

Darren nodded.

"I see that you don't believe me, but that is understandable. Even in a country as great as America, you have never seen anything like this. Tomorrow my father is coming here to show his magic in the courtyard, and then you will see that Africans may be poor, but we have special powers." When she glanced over his shoulder, he said, "All right. This is a special price for you only. Thirteen thousand C.F.A. It's all settled."

A gendarme stomped into the room, pushing a drunk ahead of him. "Jaraffe!" the drunk shouted. The boy jumped up to run from the room, but the drunk lunged and punched him in the face. Then Jaraffe's mother came forward and with one smooth swing of her arm she struck the drunk in the temple. He slid down in the gendarme's arms, his head hanging to one side, his mouth open. "Voilà!" cried the gendarme, who was also drunk. He shouted gaily in Bambara as he dragged his prisoner across the floor and propped him against the wall like a sack of millet. The woman crossed her arms over her chest again and said nothing. Again, the gendarme cried, "Voilà!" He was a handsome, barrel-chested man in a khaki uniform, with skin as black and gleaming as the pistol that hung in the holster slung around his hips. He turned his attention to Darren. "Excuse us, Madame!" he roared. "Bonsoir, Madame Américaine? Ou Madame Française? I hope we are not disturbing you."

"C'est Madame Américaine," she said firmly.

"Monsieur Gendarme. Enchanté." He thrust his hand forward. "Bière!" he shouted, and dropped down on the bench beside her. "Are you in Oulaba to visit our spectacular cliffs?"

"No," she said. "I was on my way to Timbuktu. I was going to fly out of Mopti, but —" She stopped, remembering that he was a gendarme. In Mopti, the police discovered that she wasn't carrying the *license de photographie* they required of all foreigners with cameras. The fine for this crime was the camera itself or jail. Using the alibi that she was going back to her hotel to get the permit, she had jumped into the first available jitney, ending up in Oulaba, a town that wasn't even on her map. Now she forced a thin smile. "This boy, Jaraffe, offered to be my guide. Do you know him?"

"You want Jaraffe? I'll sell him cheap." He slammed his fist down on the table, shaking Darren's bottle, and threw his head back to laugh.

"Is he a bandit?"

"No! I can't sell bandits cheap. The bandits are expensive!" He howled at his own joke and then composed himself.

"C'est Madame Américaine, ou Mademoiselle?"

"C'est Madame."

"I like your hat, Madame," he said, peering under the brim at her face. "Give it to me."

"Tomorrow," she said.

"Ah, you know Africa too well!" He shouted for Jaraffe. The doorway to the bar remained empty. "The boy is ashamed," said the gendarme. He took a drink and turned the bottle around in his broad hand. For a moment his brow creased into deep lines. His voice became maudlin. "That's the boy's father," he said, inclining his head to the drunk on the floor.

Darren turned to look at the man slumped against the wall. His torn robe was soiled to the uniform gray of fools' rags, and the nails on his hands were twisted and yellow, like the nails of a madman. A thin line of blood dribbled from his slack mouth.

Three whores dressed in tight miniskirts and stiletto heels walked into the room. They laughed at Darren in her hat.

One of them sat beside her and said, "You are my sister." She reeked of beer and cheap perfume, and her painted mouth was frightening. Darren motioned to Jaraffe's mother, who led her across the courtyard and down the corridor to a door she opened with a skeleton key. The room had a concrete floor and walls, and near the ceiling there was one tiny window with no pane, crossed with iron bars. The foam mattress on the floor was covered with a dirty *pagne.* "Merci, ma mère," said Darren. The woman tucked Darren's two bills in her bra. Talking rapidly in Bambara, she locked and unlocked the door several times, and Darren nodded. "Yes, I'll lock it," she said in English. "Thanks."

In the morning, in the bloody light of the rising sun, Darren saw the cliffs for the first time. They rose up and shimmered all around the dusty village like huge gold nuggets piled by the hands of giants. No matter where she turned she saw the low, golden mountains, scintillating in the sun like broken glass. They drew her toward them. Reason told her that mountains are farther away and higher than they seem, that she was an inexperienced climber and would not be safe out there alone; but, although Darren always put on a great show of being practical in front of other people, when left to her own devices she was as hapless as a child alone on the moon.

Her only concern was that Jaraffe might find her and insist on being her guide, so she shouldered her pack and hurried down the road. She stopped at the market to stock up on whatever seemed edible: dried dates, canned sardines, a strange fruit that rattled when she shook it. "Cheese?" she asked. "Bread?" But the women just shook their heads and laughed, holding out their rough palms for money. She wondered how Jaraffe had been able to get his hands on a Heineken. He was not among the pack of children who followed her to the edge of town, calling "Hey, white lady, look at me! I am your guide!"

The children escorted her to the banks of a muddy river where young women waded with their *pagnes* pulled up over their knees, balancing brightly colored plastic buckets on their heads. One of them knelt and drank. They all watched curiously as Darren pulled off her Gore-Tex hiking boots and rolled her jeans up to her knees. When she waded across with the pack on her back, they shouted to each other and laughed.

"Au revoir!" the children yelled from the bank. "A bientôt!" The bravest boys smacked their lips to make loud kissing noises as she went down the narrow, sandy path and curved out of their vision.

She had to keep herself from breaking into a run. The desert opened up all around her and she gulped the fresh air until her throat was parched. Within half an hour she began to burn. The sun bore through the sunscreen on her face and arms, resting on her soft freckled skin like a warm iron. She shifted the light pack on her shoulders and marched on, imagining telling her brothers in Tennessee about this adventure. As a child, she used to stand crying in the doorway when they left the house in their oiled hiking boots, shouldering heavy packs filled with Bunsen burners, gorp, and powdered eggs. "We girls have to stay home," her mother said, and she tried to teach Darren how to knit. What was a lap of tangled yarn compared to entrance in the horizon? When the boys came home, smelling of wood smoke, sweat, and leaves, she ripped out every stitch she had painstakingly knitted in the sweater sleeve. "I'm a prisoner!" she yelled. "I'll run away! You'll see!" Her mother told her to keep her voice down, and her brothers smirked.

As the sun rose higher, the cliffs lost their golden sheen and became hot, dry rocks. Darren had no sense of measure; the mountain could have been a thousand or ten thousand feet high, but the top of it seemed rather close to the clouds. When she began to climb, some of the rocks tipped under her weight. There was no sound but the dry scrape of her breathing and the slide of her boots.

Then the silence broke. "Darren!" a thin voice called. She looked at the bare rock all around her and up at the wide, empty sky. "Madame Darren! I am here!" Two yards away, through a wide crack in the rock, Jaraffe poked out his curly head. Her heart sank.

"Quelle bonne surprise!" he exclaimed, slithering out of the rock and landing on his feet like a cat. A purple bruise shone around one eye. "Here I was, just going along on my secret mission, all alone, and I find Madame Darren, my American friend!" He grinned from ear to ear. "And you're all red and tired, but still so beautiful. Were you frightened and lonely? Dismiss all your fears — your guide has found you."

She had been warned about this. If she refused his services out here he would follow her back to town and tell everyone that he had guided her but she refused to pay him. If she did accept him now as a guide, there would be no one to witness the bargain, and he might do the same thing.

"Where are your shoes, Jaraffe?"

He glanced down at his dusty feet as if he fully expected to find shoes there, then looked up and shrugged. His hands were as small as sparrows, and when he held them out by his sides, palms up, he appeared to be the most vulnerable little boy on earth. Suddenly she was furious.

"How much do you charge for this tour?"

At the nasty tone of her voice he raised his eyebrows in a perfect arc. He dragged one toe along the rock. "Two hundred American dollars."

She laughed, and he joined her in a child's falsetto. She raised her hand to him. "You are a child, and you will speak to me with respect!" When he ducked, she was ashamed of herself.

Out of reach, he smirked contemptuously and said, "Well of course, I am actually here on a secret mission for my father, as I explained last night, and so if you choose to follow me, well then, I assure you that you will see what no tourist ever sees. I thought you were my friend, and so I had planned to show you a sacred burial cave filled with Dogon treasure. But this obviously bores Madame. I beg her pardon."

"You lie, boy." He looked at her, and for a moment she was afraid, but she continued, raising her voice. "There is no sacred treasure, and your father is not a magician."

"You lie!" he yelled. "You don't have a husband. You lie, and also you speak French like a dog!" He stepped back from her and mocked her accent, laughing in a high whine.

"Your father isn't a magician. He's a drunk."

Blood rose to his cheeks and his eyes turned almost black. "Whore! Dog-French white-lady whore!"

"Well, you've lost your fancy manners, haven't you," she said softly in English. "You snot-nosed little brat."

For an instant he gazed at her mouth, wrinkling his smooth brow, as if the words still hung about her lips and might be grasped, but then he turned his head away. "I don't understand your language and I hope the hyenas eat you!"

"Five thousand C.F.A.," she said in French. "Fifteen American dollars. That's the price — if I see the Dogon burial cave."

He spit. Then he jumped from one rock to the next, leaping the boulders like a kid goat until he was gone.

Soon she heard his spook sounds — strange whistles and long, sad wails echoing in the caves inside the cliff. Clinging to the rock, she inched her way toward the sky. At noon, when she stopped to eat, her body trembled. Sweat stung her dry lips, salting the food as she put it in her mouth. The warm, heavily chlorinated water was delicious, and she was sorry she hadn't brought more than one canteen. She removed her hat, stretched out on the rock, and dozed.

First she sensed his presence. When he was close enough, she smelled his sweet child's sweat, already familiar.

"Six thousand C.F.A.," she said without opening her eyes. He did not answer. Instead, he touched her sunglasses and then her hair. He was leaning over her face now, so close that his breath stirred the tiny hairs in her nose. She felt the wet, exquisite curve of his lips on her ear, whispering in a strange tongue. Then she sneezed.

Abruptly, she sat up. "What is your problem?" she yelled in English. He stared at her mouth, his eyes large and dark, the purple bruise glistening. He smiled hopefully. "If this desert were hell, you'd be Satan," she said. She continued to speak in English as she busied her shaking hands with the water bottle. She gave him a drink. "Where are your shoes? Are you hungry? Here, eat." She set out the dates and the sardines. Pressed close against her legs, he began to eat with feline grace, sucking all the sugar from the fruit and all the oil from the fish, finishing everything she dropped before him.

When he had eaten his fill he said, "Seven thousand C.F.A." Without waiting for a response, he tossed her bag across his narrow back and began zigzagging up the side of the cliff. She faced the first boulder he had mounted, fingering the smooth surface for a grip. Then she jumped, catching the top of the rock with her hands, scraping her knees and elbows as she lugged herself over the edge. From a perch far above her head he looked down and said in heavily accented English, "What is your problem?"

He told her to remove the hiking boots and hang them around her neck. As they climbed, the soft pink soles of her feet became familiar with the wrinkled face of the rock, and she moved more swiftly, but no matter how quickly she climbed, Jaraffe skimmed ahead of her. His bronze legs disappeared against the rock, and his blue shirt melted into the sky. Only his black curls stood out against the horizon, and, when he turned, the flash of his smile. She did not look down.

At last, when the sun was easing down over the mountain, Jaraffe stopped to rest. She handed him her canteen and he drank half of what was left. She took two short drinks, hesitated, took a third.

"Where is this Dogon cave?"

"Here."

"Where?" There was nothing around them but rock, and, far below, the tiny squiggle of a sand path cutting through a velvet desert. When she climbed around the rock where they were resting, she saw a field cut in furrows as thin as pencil marks, dotted with Dogon farmers.

He rolled over and grabbed her ankles, whispering, "Come back, you fool. The Dogons will see you. We are on sacred ground!"

She edged herself back against the wall. "Don't grab me," she said, whispering back despite herself. "I am older than you. Respect me."

"The dead are older than you. Respect them."

"Shut up."

"Shut up," he mimicked in English.

She lowered herself into a sitting position, keeping her back to the stone. For the first time it occurred to her that they wouldn't be able to get back down the cliff before nightfall. Her hand played with the cap of the canteen, twisting it back and forth.

"I'm going into the cave," he said. "You may follow me if you so desire. In the case of catastrophe, you are not my responsibility. I'm just informing you. Americans like to know these things beforehand."

"Jaraffe, we have to spend the night up here. You told me we could make the climb in one day."

"Maybe I will find you some beautiful earrings, or some money. But if you are complaining I won't give the present to you. Then I will give it to one of my other girlfriends, or perhaps I'll keep it for myself."

She ignored the girlfriend reference. "We need water," she said.

"I am going on my secret mission." He rolled his eyes in cool mystery. "Are you coming?"

The entrance to the cave was blocked by a boulder. "Otherwise," Jaraffe explained, "the hyenas would eat the corpses." They stood on either side of it and rolled it away. Jaraffe asked for Darren's flashlight, peering over her shoulder as she dug in her pack for it. He switched it on, dropped to his hands and knees, and crawled behind a scraggly bush. A second later, Darren knelt down, too. She followed the pink soles of his feet into the tunnel, slapping her hands over the thin edge of light that moved behind him. She could smell something rancid, like rotting steak. Jaraffe began to hum. The hum reverberated in the narrow shaft, sounding in her bones as she and Jaraffe wound down into the belly of the mountain. Then they turned the last corner, and Jaraffe stood up and moved the circle of light around the room.

It was filled with human skeletons. They were stacked from the floor to the ceiling. Some of them were seated along the walls, behind urns full of beads and trinkets. The flashlight threw quivering strips of light into stark eye-holes, gaping jaws, and the thick spaces between yellow ribs. The room stank.

Jaraffe sang. It was a low, mournful tune, full of strange notes and nonsensical words. They stood beside a pile of corpses. The bottom of the heap was nothing but dust, and the human form seemed to rise out of this, a shoulder pushing up, a jaw jutting out, a broken hand digging back down into the powder. In the middle of the stack the skeletons were complete; at the top, near the ceiling, scraps of faded *pagnes* hung off the bones. It was as though the corpses on top had grown out of the dead beneath them. It was as though Darren and Jaraffe, panting and sweating, had rolled off the top of the heap, obscenely alive.

Jaraffe slid behind the pile, leaving her in darkness. She heard him rattling in the bones but she did not follow. Once his light shot across the room, illuminating a skeleton sitting cross-legged against the wall, holding an urn between its knees. Inside the urn, besides beads and a few C.F.A. coins, there was a rusted can opener. She felt despair. What hand was cruel enough to create a human being, a sad fool who could see his end, and then smash him to dust? The light was dimming. "Jaraffe, don't burn out the batteries," she called softly, and the sound of her voice frightened her.

"Oui, j'arrive!" He rummaged noisily in the pile of skeletons, shaking the fingers on the hands, the toes on the feet, turning the heads this way and that. His hum was high, loud, and uncertain. At last he scurried back to her. "Come! Hurry!" He dropped down on all fours and sped up the shaft. Darren followed, knocking her head against the ceiling, scraping her knees, senseless to the pain.

Outside, the sun fell in graceful surrender to the night, throwing out its last miracles as it cloaked the jagged edge of the horizon in shadow. Birds sang myriad unearthly notes, brazenly breaking the day's long silence. In the dying sun, Jaraffe's bare arms and legs turned gold. When he stood on the ledge holding the skeleton of a human hand like a scepter over the Dogon farmers in the fields below, he looked like a god. A few farmers still bent over their short, primitive hoes, but most of them had thrown the shafts over their shoulders and were walking toward the mountain. Their villages were built so cleverly into the sides of the cliffs that one could walk right by them and never see a human dwelling. Like the birds, the farmers had begun to sing out to each other.

"Forgive me for calling you a liar this morning," Darren said. "I'm glad that you're my guide." He turned his head to hide the frank pleasure on his face.

"This is the cave where we will sleep tonight," he said, motioning to an overhanging rock. "I hope it pleases you."

She crawled inside. The ceiling was so low she couldn't stand up, but the floor was large enough for the two of them to stretch out when they slept. A hollow in the back wall led to other passages that were too dark to see.

"Jaraffe," she called, stepping out onto the ledge, "I think there are too many openings; something could come —" She stopped. He had opened her pack. The camera hung around his neck and he was rubbing a stick of deodorant along his face. His nostrils flared delicately as he sniffed the scent.

She snatched the deodorant out of his hand. "Do not ever open my pack without my permission!"

He hunched his shoulders together and then lifted his chin. "I don't care. Mosquitoes don't bite Africans if they can bite white ladies."

"What?" She burst into laughter. "That's not mosquito repellent. That's deodorant; it goes under your arms. Oh, never mind." She pulled the camera off his neck and tried to take his picture, but he turned his back to her.

"You don't have anything good to eat in your pack," he grumbled. "The other Americans had chocolate, and macaroni and cheese. You don't even have a stove."

"You aren't required to eat with me." As she knelt beside him, putting the items back into the pack, she smelled the deodorant on his face and chuckled. "I'm sorry, Jaraffe. It's just that it's funny to Americans."

With her army knife, he cut a string from her roll of twine and tied the skeleton hand around his neck. "The other Americans had Kool-Aid as well. Grape." He held up the fruit she had bought in the market and looked at it with disgust before he cut off the top. "Beggars' food," he snorted, sliding two fingers inside the hard shell and popping a fleshy seed into his mouth. "Food for lepers."

"Where's the water?"

"Africans don't need water."

"Well, Americans do." She turned up the canteen he had nearly emptied.

"Americans carry extra batteries," he said. She tried to turn the flashlight on; the batteries were dead. He smiled and handed her the fruit. The sweet and sour seed puckered her lips and burned her stomach, but the juice soothed her thirst. He laughed at her grimaces.

"Are you cold?" she asked.

"Africans don't get cold."

She tossed a sweater at his head and carried her own warm clothes to the cave to change. When she looked back, he was smelling the sweater, running his fingers over the cashmere and sliding it along his cheek. Inside the cave, something rustled. Wind? She couldn't make herself crawl inside. With her back turned, she changed her clothes and returned to sit beside him.

Black curls fell across his forehead and his eyes gleamed yellow in the falling darkness. The sweater swallowed him. The cuffs flapped below his hands as he crossed his arms and commented, "Your body is very beautiful, but I find your derrière too small."

"Shut up, Jaraffe."

"I see that you are frightened to go in our cave, or perhaps you have fallen in love with me."

The muscles in her back tensed. "You? You are a child!" His face stiffened in humiliation. He began to hum.

The stars came out in rapid succession, crowding the huge black sky until they nearly touched each other. She lay on her back looking for Sirius, the great star of the Dogons.

When she gazed too long at the sky, she lost all sense of direction and had to press her hands flat against the cold rock. Behind her the gaping mouth of the cave waited, and she dreaded it. The boy seemed a stranger to her now, chanting his lonely, foreign hymns, accompanying the sole bird that remained awake. The birdcall was like nothing she had ever heard. It wasn't a screech or a caw or the notes of a song, but something chilling and abrupt, like the scream of a woman.

"Jaraffe, what is that bird?"

"There is no bird."

"Yes, listen. It screams like a woman." It screamed then, louder than before. "That one."

"That's a hyena."

"Where is the hyena?"

"It's here." The scream came again, and her heart pounded. "She smells your fear," he added reproachfully.

"Aren't you afraid?"

"I am the son of a magician, do you forget so quickly? I went into the sacred Dogon grave and took my talisman." He rattled the fingers on the skeleton hand. "The hyena is afraid of me."

"What happens if the hyena comes into the cave while we're sleeping?"

She heard him yawn. A bank of clouds rolled across the sky, and the stars blinked out, one by one, like lights going off in a house.

"You aren't earning your keep as a guide," she said.

"Ha! Ha, ha. I am a child, remember? I am a child when Madame decides that I am to be a child. Now Madame is afraid and needs a man. Am I to be a man now?"

He reached for her breast, laughing when she knocked his hand away. "A child, then. Well, the child is going to bed. Sweet dreams, Madame."

She lay on her back looking up at the sky until the last star blinked out. Then it was terribly dark, and cold. Every sound — the rustle of weeds, the roll of gravel, the rasping of her own breath — was magnified until her nerves were taut with fear. She saw the empty stare of the skeletons. When the hyena screamed again she jumped up and ran to the mouth of the cave.

"Jaraffe?" He did not answer. She leaned down and pushed her head through the opening, blinking in the darkness. "I'm not coming in until you answer me." Suddenly, something swished behind her. With a thud, the animal landed on her back. She screamed.

"Waa!" Jaraffe cried, rolling off her back, doubled over in laughter. He leaped about her, pulling his hair, rolling his eyes, crying out in sharp female wails. "Waa!" he cried. "Oh, oh, help me! Where is my big, strong, handsome guide?"

With her heart still knocking in her chest, she swung her fist at him. He ducked it like a boxer. "Damn you!" she yelled. He shrieked — a scared, mean laugh. She lunged for him and caught hold of his skinny arm, but he slipped out of her grasp. For a moment they stood facing each other in the dark, panting, and then she hissed, "I despise you." She began to sob in broken screams that scraped her throat raw. It was a horrible, lonely sound. She covered her mouth, choking in the effort to stop the noise. She felt his presence somewhere in front of her, small and no longer fierce, and she crawled into the cave. She made a thin pallet from the rest of the clothes in her pack and lay down, first on her back, then on her stomach. Then she rolled over on her back again. Each lump in the rock made a distinct stab into her flesh. She began to wonder about Jaraffe and to want him with her, if only to slap him.

A few minutes later, he scooted into the cave. "And where is my bed?" he demanded. She remained silent. "You are angry with me." He stretched out beside her on the hard floor and pushed her arm. "Say something, Darren, my dear friend Darren." When she rolled away from him, he patted her head like a baby. "You were crying, and I did not help you. Now I have scared you. You are so good to me, giving me food and water and this sweater. I do not even like grape Kool-Aid and macaroni and cheese and chocolate — well, maybe chocolate. I like the sweater; it keeps me warm and smells very nice." He gave a loud, appreciative sniff.

"You annoy me."

"This is true. I am annoying and rude and bad. I am ugly." He waited for her to contradict this last statement, and when she did not, he continued. "Many people share your opinion. It is all true." He let his voice become pitiful. "Surely I will burn in hell. Or Allah will find some way to punish me, so that I never forget my sins against you and am always ashamed."

Despite herself, she spoke. "When I first met you, last night, I thought, here is a boy different from all the other little bandits in Africa. Here is a serious boy. Now I see that I was mistaken. You are just like all the other scoundrels in the street."

"My remorse is more enormous than the sky."

"You are not sincere."

"This is true. I am sorry. Will you forgive me?"

She tossed him the roll of pants and shirts that had been her pillow and closed her eyes. Noisily, he made his bed beside her and continued his apology. His voice purred against the cold, black walls. He spoke nonsense. At last, he lay down against her back, throwing an arm around her neck and sticking his cold feet between her calves.

"I don't like that, Jaraffe. Stop it."

"I don't have any socks. My feet are cold."

"You can take some socks out of my pack." She listened as he rummaged through her things, mumbling to himself in various tongues, and then she felt him once again press his small hard body against her back. When his arm circled her neck, the skeleton hand, still tied around his neck, cut between her shoulder blades. "You will take me with you back to America, and I will go to medical school and become a great surgeon . . ." he murmured sleepily in her ear. "We will get married . . . and have a big house in Dallas, Texas."

She fell into a light sleep nettled with nightmares and awoke strangling in his skinny arms. His breath shot out in hard, quick pants, and his heart, racing against her own, knocked on her chest. Above them, the hyena's scream tangled with the anguished shrieking of another animal. The beasts thrashed and rolled on the roof of the cave, knocking pebbles and clumps of dirt through the cracks. Jaraffe's arms gripped her like thin iron rods. His heart was banging so hard in his chest that she thought he would explode. She hugged the clinging boy tighter against her, hiding her face in his hair, and thought, *I will live. I will.* For a long time they lay in their rigid embrace, listening to the hyena chew its shrieking victim. The boy's glowing yellow eyes made the only light in the cave.

When Darren awoke, Jaraffe was gone. He had taken her camera and her hat with him. The leather purse hanging around her neck was flat and empty. Even her passport was gone. "Bastard!" she screamed out over the desert. "Thief!" She threw a rock over the side of the cliff, and then another, screaming as tears ran down her cheeks. She didn't want to climb back down into the world, not ever, but Jaraffe had drunk all of her water and her tongue was swollen with thirst. She shouldered the pack and began to back slowly down the cliff.

By nightfall Darren was back at the Grand Hotel du Mali. Jaraffe's mother stood in the doorway of the bar, watching her stagger, hatless, dirty, ragged, across the courtyard. Silently, the hotelkeeper went behind the bar and handed Darren a beer. Then, without expression, she wet a towel, and, leaning forward, roughly scrubbed Darren's face and hands. Darren stood still, in shock; then she sat down at the table and ate the plate of macaroni and tough, greasy meat the woman brought to her. When she pushed her plate back she saw the passport under it. "They're all cunning," she said softly, and pushed the small blue book into her bra. Then she waited for Jaraffe. While she waited, she drank beer. Each time she took a fresh bottle of Gazelle from Jaraffe's mother, she felt a new surge of power. *I'll kill him,* she thought.

Around ten o'clock Jaraffe sauntered into the bar, wearing a new white suit and a shirt the color of lemons. Darren's brown felt hat was tilted at a rakish angle on his head. A cigarette dangled from his lips. After a brief moment when it looked as though he might run back out the door, he flashed his best grin and said, "Darren, *ma chérie,* at last I find you! Oh, at last!" She waited. She let him swagger to her. As he bent down to touch his lips to her cheek in the French manner, she smelled alcohol and cheap perfume. "Why did you worry me like this? I thought you were lost forever." When he leaned forward to kiss her other cheek, she grabbed his neck. She pressed her fingers into the soft skin, digging them in between the tendons, and shook him until her hat fell off his head. His strangled cries filled the room. "Mama!" he yelled. "Help me!"

His mother came and stood silently before them. "Help!"

cried Jaraffe, and the gendarme ran out from the back room, buckling his pants. Then the doorway filled with whores and men, shouting and pushing against each other to get into the room.

"He stole my money!" Darren yelled.

"I did not. This woman hired me to be her guide. I took her into the cliffs, as she asked me to, and then she paid me and told me to go. I gave the money to my mother, who needs it to take care of my poor father." The crowd pressed noisily into the room and around Darren. One of the whores pushed her painted face down close and whispered, "He's a thief, that one." Darren felt the prostitute's long nails rest briefly on her arm. Jaraffe's mother stared straight at the wall.

The gendarme looked into Darren's eyes. "I will help you," he said. He laid his broad hand on her shoulder. "Have confidence in me." His hand moved slowly upward until his fingers rested in her hair. She shook it off wearily. "You are an educated woman, eh? You know many things? Some languages? You know perhaps how to drive a car? You know how to work a computer? Many, many things live in this head." He rolled his hand over her head as if it were a coconut. "Your head is no good here, eh?" He picked the hat up off the floor and pushed it gently down over her ears, as if to stop her from thinking. Then he snapped his fingers at Jaraffe's mother.

The woman brought two beers; then, from inside her bra, she took a roll of soft bills and laid them silently before Darren. Jaraffe swaggered over and set down her camera. Darren waited a moment to see if the gendarme meant to demand her permit. The man grinned at her, then turned away and drank up, and she stuffed the camera into her bag.

In the morning she took a jitney back to Bamako, and all along the way, young boys begged to guide her.

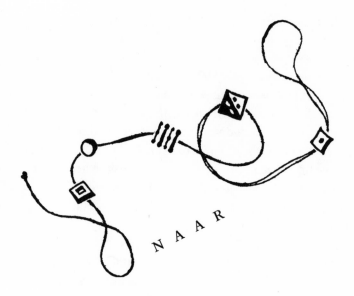

N A A R

A *naar* lay naked across the road in front of the white van. Darren stared through the windshield at the Arab. She had never seen more than their long brown hands — passing eggs and light bulbs over a dusty counter, cupping money, sliding a knife across the throat of a ram — and their eyes, dark and impenetrable between the folds of a scarf. When they walked, their robes billowed out like sails; she never saw feet. The robes were like houses they wore on their backs, and sometimes she had wanted to poke them like turtles. The Arab lay on his back with his arms tied behind his head; someone had cut off his penis.

When she braked the car, three of the Senegalese boys jumped up on the hood, pressing their angry faces flat against the glass. The others swarmed around the car, beating on the roof with their hands and staring into the windows. Darren's hair, dark at the roots, still showed the yellow streaks of Belle Lady hair coloring, and, having lost her contacts long ago, she now wore thick, tortoiseshell glasses that turned dark in the sunlight.

"Descendez!" they cried. She could neither remove her hand from the steering wheel nor hit the accelerator. As a man pushed through the crowd with a stone, she unrolled her window, leaving a space too narrow for a hand to reach in and unlock the door. They pushed their faces in closer. One of the boys on the hood held up the bloody penis for her to see. Keeping one hand firmly gripped on the steering wheel, she took a cigarette and handed the rest of the pack through the window. A crazed laughter ran through the crowd. Her hand shook so hard that the flame of her lighter went out again.

"Naar!" a voice called. The laughing stopped.

"You know I'm not a *naar*," she said in French. "A *naar* is a Mauritanian, and this is a war between the Senegalese and the Mauritanians. I am American."

"Excuse-nous, *toubab!*" a boy shouted, and the crowd laughed again. *Toubab* meant white nigger, like *naar* meant Arab nigger.

"My name is Fatou," she said. She imagined them picking the car up and turning it over, throwing the stone through the window at her head, so she began to lie.

"My husband is Senegalese. We have a baby, a boy." She was talking to the boy in the window who looked older only because he wasn't wearing sunglasses. He smoked one of her cigarettes, looking back at her. Behind him, the others argued in Wolof.

It had begun two days earlier with a cow. On the Senegalese/Mauritanian border, a cow was stolen. War rose like the sun across the desert, burning into every village, every hut, every heart, exploding in the capital of Dakar. This morning the Mauritanians had sent a planeload of mutilated Senegalese into Dakar — some of them were still alive. Again the cry rose up in the crowd, "*Naar!*" The sweat on her neck felt cold.

"What is your husband's name?" the boy without sunglasses asked.

She looked into his brown eyes. "Yousouf Tall," she said softly, naming the first friend that came to mind, a colleague at the university where she taught English.

"Give me your sunglasses."

"They are prescription glasses. You can't see with them."

"Give them to me," he said, elbowing the others out of the way. Without the glasses she saw only a blur of color.

"You're blind," he said, handing them back to her. He turned and began yelling something to the others. A shout rose up as the boys circled around the van, blocking it from all sides except where the *naar* lay. "You can go," said the boy at the window. "Drive over him and go."

She shut her eyes and shifted the van into gear. It was like going over a speed bump, except for the crunching that went straight to her teeth. Not until the front tires were on his body did it occur to her that he might not have been dead. "Go!" the boys cried, beating on the back of the car. She stepped down on the accelerator, pushing it all the way to the floor, swerving out toward the swift, thin black bodies, the people who had done this for what was done to them, and careening down the road.

Along the road the flames from black and gutted cars licked up toward the sun, turned white, and shimmered. Balls of smoke hung in the sky. Darren drove past hordes of women running down the street, holding their *pagnes* around their waists with one hand, babies jouncing on their backs. Children streamed around them, laughing and crying. A Senegalese tank rolled by, scattering some sheep who ran first one way and then the other, their heads jerking up, eyes rolling back with terror. *There are riots downtown,* she thought, *and they've brought out the military. These languid people have gone mad, during the holy month of Ramadan, in daylight, when a Muslim cannot eat or drink or*

*make love or think impure thoughts, when the men walk down
the street spitting so as not to swallow their saliva and break the
fast.* She had drunk a cold glass of water in front of Yousouf,
watching him spit. "Drink," he said. "These aren't your rules."

Her stomach tightened at the whistle of the gas bombs, waiting for the crack. Even with the windows shut, the gas got into
the car and made tears run down her cheeks. She felt it in her
nose and in her head; it split her thoughts like mercury.

In front of her apartment she carefully parked the Peace Corps
van and locked the door. Without looking back at the tires, she
walked under the big leafy trees to the courtyard where the
guards were praying on their mats, their bows and arrows leaning against the wall. Halfway up the stairs she stopped and
vomited over the railing. She could not make herself go inside
the quiet, empty apartment. She wanted to hold someone and
thought of Yousouf, but he was not her lover. Even if he were
her lover, he could not so much as shake her hand until the sun
set and the fast was over for the day. She stood in the corridor,
wiping her face with a bandana, then turned and went back
down the stairs, out of the courtyard, and into the street.

A crowd had gathered along the edge of the wide avenue. Boys
ran in the street, pulling empty cigarette cartons by long strings
while they made sounds like trucks with their mouths. She watched
their hard, thin bodies running in the bright sun; their faces wore
expressions of intense concentration. She wanted to take one of
the boys in her arms, feel his panting chest, and look into his
round, intelligent eyes.

"Toubab!" a boy called to her and ran away giggling. His
friends echoed him as she walked around the corner to the shop.
The door of the wooden shed hung broken on its hinge; the glass
case inside was smashed and empty. She remembered that the
Mauritanian shopkeeper's name was Mohammed, and that she
had not liked him because he once refused to give her thirty

C.F.A. worth of credit for some candy. At the Senegalese shop next door she asked the man behind the counter what had happened to Mohammed.

He shrugged. A woman holding a girl on her hip looked at her and said nothing.

"He's dead," the child offered. When her mother smacked her, a great wail rose out of her little pink mouth, then she stopped suddenly, looking out from thick wet lashes at Darren, as if the scream had come from her. Darren bought her a piece of candy. She bought one of each of the items on the shelf. The man put everything into a plastic sack and handed it to her, keeping his eyes on the money in her hand.

"You're going to hide," he said.

"Why do I have to hide? Look at me. I am white, not brown. I am not a *naar.*"

"That is true," he said, "but war is blind." He and the woman laughed; the child chimed in a second later.

As she stepped onto the street she felt again the sensation of bones crunching beneath her. She walked to the bread kiosk, bought a baguette, and lingered there, leaning against the tin shelf, chewing on the warm loaf wrapped in newspaper. The crowd on the avenue was silent.

"What's going on?" The man inside the kiosk would not meet her eyes or answer. "I am not a *naar,*" she said. People were staring at her, and she suddenly realized that she was the only foreigner in the street. She stuffed the rest of the loaf into her sack and walked into the crowd at the edge of the avenue. "Bonjour," she said, pressing in close to a large, beautiful woman in bright yellow gauze who was cleaning her teeth with a chew stick. The woman smelled faintly of peanuts. The street was empty except for a tank at the far end, but the crowd stood waiting for something.

"What's happening?"

"I don't know," the woman said.

A soldier with a machine gun slung over his shoulder weaved between them. Her heart beat fast, and she stared down at the ground until he was gone. The people pressed in closer together; she felt the warmth of someone leaning against her shoulder, smelled the rich blend of perfumes and sweats, and could not make herself go back into the white, empty apartment. If she went to Yousouf's house, what would she say? "I'm scared?" or "Marry me?"

A child pulled at her arm. "Madame," he said in careful French, "you must hide." When she did not move he pulled her arm again and repeated, "You must hide," and then, throwing one reproachful look over his shoulder, he was gone.

It happened fast. A hand clutched at her face, tore, and the glasses were gone. The bag was snatched out of her hand. She saw the blue back of a boy who had been standing next to her streak through the blur of colors. "Thief!" she cried. "Your mother is a whore!" The crowd stirred, turning to look at her.

"Go home," a man said, but now the crowd was between her and the apartment building. She turned and went in the opposite direction, toward the tank. A grenade whistled, the sound growing high and thin, then dropping down into the crowd behind her. Faceless soldiers swam around the tank. Since she could not see them clearly she felt less visible herself.

Avenue Pompidou was empty. Down in the side streets more grenades exploded, echoed by children's firecrackers. In front of her, red and green blobs floated in the air.

"Madame! Balloons? Balloons for the madame?"

He was a little man with a creased face and orange teeth. The balloons were all tied to his left arm; when he talked he waved the arm, making the sky above him whorl softly in color.

"I don't want a balloon. This isn't a party; it's a war. Are you crazy?"

"For you, my friend, six hundred francs." He took her wrist and tied the balloon to it.

"One hundred francs."

"What!" he exclaimed, pulling her back by the string.

"Take it off! I don't want it."

"It won't come off! You wanted it, and I tied it to you, so now you have to pay for it. Five hundred and fifty francs."

"It's not enough that I'm white," she said, angrily. "Now you tie a balloon on me, just in case somebody is a bad shot."

"Marry me, and I will protect you." He grinned.

"I'm already married."

"Is he Senegalese?"

"Yes." At that moment she knew where she was going. Dropping the money into his palm, she went down the street with the balloon sailing behind her. Once Yousouf had taken her to his aunt's house for lunch; afterward he took her to his apartment, where they watched TV. When he tried to kiss her, she had turned her head away.

"Just on the cheek," he had said. His smile was beautiful. "One."

She had stepped away from him. Two days later at work when they were alone on the elevator he kissed her nose; she hadn't spoken to him since then. What would she say now? "Salut, Yousouf. Ça va? You know me." Her eyes began to hurt, straining to recognize the street.

She took a left when a man began to follow her and started walking as fast as possible. He moved toward her in a blur, a tall young man with a deep voice. "Madame," he called softly. Down the street a shouting arose, followed by the stamping of feet. Behind her the man called, "Madame, I want to talk to you." The street was narrow, winding, and filled with empty doorways. *I might die today,* she thought, and her body ached with the energy to live. "Madame," the unctuous voice called, closer now. "I know you."

She ran. The balloon seemed to pull her back. Ahead the shouting rose to a shrill pitch, and something shot up the hill toward her. At first she thought it was a car, then, a bicycle. It came flying at her — two boys rolling an empty wheelchair, one boy holding on to each handle. Their screams were taut with ecstasy.

Sprinting, she willed her legs to go faster, opening her mouth wider as the air cut into her lungs. The world was spinning by so fast that all the colors ran together into a muddy brown. In her mind there was only the will to go faster and the image of Yousouf's door, of his face and hands, the rocking of his voice.

The young man was still running behind her, his feet slapping on the pavement. When she turned her head around to see him, she ran into the broad chest of another man. She tried to dodge around him, but he hooked her around the waist with one arm and pulled her inside a bar. She gritted her teeth against a wave of nausea and felt again the crunching of bones under tires. The iron gate clanked down and locked.

"Fatou," the man said, shaking her gently. "Don't be afraid. Don't you remember me? I'm Bouba. This is Chez Bouba, the bar, you know? This is my bar. You came here once and we were speaking some English together, yes? Those boys chase you, and I kill them." He smacked his fist into his palm and laughed.

"I lost my glasses. I can't see."

"No! Ndeysaan! You will take a beer. How do you say, under the house?"

"On the house. Thanks."

Beads of sweat formed on the green glass bottle and melted between her fingers. She swallowed. Bouba sat next to her, lighting a cigarette for her and then one for himself. She held her hands over her eyes, rubbing them. He yelled for someone to open the gate.

"No problem now, that boy is gone."

"I was going to see my husband; he lives down the street from here."

"Ah, you have gotten married? Senegalese or American?"

"Senegalese." Leaning back in the chair, drinking the cold beer, she closed her eyes and imagined Yousouf's smooth mahogany face that was cut at angles, the slanting eyes, the delicate curve of his lips. Then she thought of dying.

"I can hear your heart!" Bouba said. "You run fast."

"I want to see my husband."

When someone called, "Bouba!" he turned and ambled toward the bar. After a moment, a man sat down beside her.

"Bonjour."

She nodded, keeping her hand over her eyes. His breath smelled strongly of fish. When he poked her arm, she opened her eyes and turned reluctantly toward him, frowning. He was wearing a dirty white robe with a red stocking cap and sunglasses. From his pocket he removed what appeared to be a rock. He held it under her nose and shook it until two scaly legs appeared. A long withered neck slid out. "Want to buy a turtle?" he asked, trying to pull the tail out with his free hand.

"Get lost," she said, turning away.

"For you, my friend, twenty thousand C.F.A."

"Look, I don't want a turtle. Leave me alone." She imagined its ugly head drawn into the dark hole of its shell, the glittering eyes pressed back into the wrinkled folds of its neck.

"For you, sixteen thousand C.F.A."

"You come in here and see this white person, this *toubab*," she said, her voice rising, "and thank your lucky stars you've found someone stupid enough to buy a turtle! Who wants a turtle? What does a person do with a turtle? Huh?"

"You insult me," he said, waving the turtle in front of her face. "Many white people buy turtles. They keep them in their salons and watch them grow."

"Wonderful."

"Give me a cigarette."

"No." When she stood up to walk over to the bar he pulled her back by the balloon string. She jerked it back, watching the hideous grin spread over his face.

"Hey! You get out of here!" Bouba called out in Wolof. "Leave her alone. Fatou, come up to the bar and take a beer. Tu n'es pas contente."

She was leaning on the bar, standing next to a man asleep with his head in his arms, when she smelled the turtle man again.

"You pay me ten thousand C.F.A.," he said, sitting the turtle on her shoulder.

"Get out," she said.

"Naar," he whispered, pushing the turtle toward her neck.

Bouba came around the bar. He raised his hand and hit the man in the head. He didn't watch him shuffle out. "Now," he said, "I will take you home to your husband and you will be happy again." The man who was sleeping next to her didn't move. Bouba led Darren outside, where he pulled the gate back down and locked it.

"There's still a man at the bar," she said.

"He is my father. Leave him there. His sister was on the plane from Nouakchott and he is too sad to move."

A small crowd that had gathered around the turtle man shouted at Bouba as he led her down the street, but he paid no attention.

"It is a sin to kill," he was saying, "and this is the holy month of Ramadan. God is not happy. Men are fools, and I am a man — today I could kill. This is all madness, have you seen it before?"

"No, I've never seen this before."

"This is how you grow into an old woman." He followed her into the courtyard, smoking a cigarette and talking.

Her heart jumped when she saw the door open. Quickly she

combed her fingers through her hair and straightened the belt around her dress. For the first time she wondered if Yousouf would love her.

"You are nice now," Bouba said, "but there is some dirt on your face." She took the bandana he offered, wiped her face with it, and squeezed it into a ball.

A maid stepped out of the door with a broom. She and Bouba spoke to each other in Wolof.

"He's gone," Bouba said, turning to Fatou. "You will wait."

"Tell the maid to leave now, and I'll lock the door and wait."

"Why do *toubabs* like to be alone?"

"We don't ride on our mothers' backs when we're babies."

"Even the babies have cars in America."

She smiled. "My husband will be here soon."

"I do not hear your heart now," he said. "You are home."

When he was gone she locked the door and undressed, tearing the balloon off her wrist. It floated up gently and rolled across the ceiling. After a shower she pulled on a shirt and a pair of shorts that she found folded across the back of a chair. She liked the smell of Yousouf's shirt. Her eyes throbbed from the strain of trying to see; she rolled Bouba's bandana into a blindfold and tied it over her eyes.

The bombs began again. From within his house they were like music, and she was ashamed to find them beautiful. "I killed a man," she said aloud in the empty room, and waited. She didn't care. Later it would rise up like a welt on her soul, and scar, but now she couldn't feel it. She wanted to eat and drink and make love, because she was alive. Soon she would undress Yousouf and feel his supple young body, all intact, pulsing with unshed blood. When they fell asleep she would not let go and not for one single moment of the night would she be alone. She lay across the bed with her arms folded behind her head, listening for his footstep between the bombs.

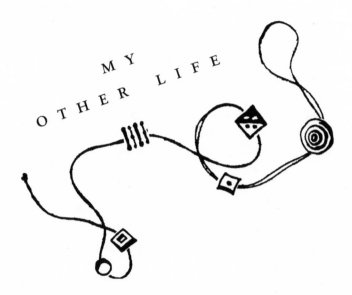

MY OTHER LIFE

In Africa, I often imagined that my parents were dead. Although my mother sent me long letters and my father wrote on the backs of her pages, signing his name beside a Martian face that he colored in with his highlighter, Jessie Ray and Dean had receded so far back into my mind that I pictured them as midgets. They had the bluish white skin of zombies, and, like the people in my dreams, they spoke with their mouths closed. When I pretended they were dead, I got drunk and cried for hours. Then, lying on the cool black and white tiles of my living room floor, with the batiks and wooden masks spinning slowly around me, I fantasized about my wedding with Yousouf Ibrahima Tall.

We would be married at the First Baptist Church in Stipple, Tennessee. Since Yousouf was the son of a man with three wives and twenty-one children, our engagement announcement would take up a full page of the Stipple *Star News*. Everyone would be horrified. They would flock to the wedding and crane their necks to see Darren Parkman say "I do" and kiss a man as black as Satan.

His beauty would outrage them. He was slender, long-limbed, and high-gloss black all over except for his palms and the soles of his feet, which were pink. His lips were a deeper pink, cut into a wet, exquisite curve. He had a straight nose, flaring delicately at the nostrils, and enormous eyes so thickly lashed that they appeared to be lined with kohl. I pictured him walking down the aisle — smooth, catlike — and hoped someone would faint.

Even in my wildest moments I could not imagine my parents at this ceremony. Two years ago at the Memphis airport, Dean had made me promise him that I would not come home with a Senegalese man.

"I haven't asked you for many things in your life," he said, "but promise me this: Promise your dad that you won't marry a black man."

"Peace Corps volunteers aren't allowed to fraternize with the natives," I said, but he looked all the way into me with his blue eyes, and I promised.

When I realized that I loved Yousouf, I stopped answering my door. He came to my apartment at different times of the day and night, trying to catch me at home. I always waited until I heard his footsteps growing faint on the stairs before I bent down to pick up his note. Then one day I opened the door. It had never been locked.

Although he kept a room on the outskirts of Dakar, where rent was cheaper, Yousouf spent most of his time at my apartment. I made it clear to him that I would never give him a key, and it took him three months to get one off of me. After a year, we began to talk about marriage.

"The reason I won't marry you," I told him, "is that I would hate your second wife." He was sitting on a Moroccan cushion, one skinny leg crossed over the other, clipping his toenails into the palm of his hand. He was naked except for a pair of black bikini briefs and the string of leather talismans he wore around his waist.

"Mais non," he said, lifting his head so that I could see the strong, clean line of his jaw. "Quelle deuxième femme?" He flashed his white teeth and assured me that it was entirely too expensive to keep more than one wife on a banker's salary in Dakar.

Once I showed him a newspaper photo of the Ku Klux Klan marching down Main Street in Stipple. "Laa laa i laa!" he exclaimed. "Xoolal góor — ñii!" I leaned over his shoulder to look at the men. Their white robes and pointed hoods resembled the costumes that nine-year-old Senegalese boys wore after their circumcisions, when they paraded in the streets. "Will these men kill me?" asked Yousouf. "Will they come to our wedding and shoot me with pistols, like the American cowboys?" He rolled his eyes to the ceiling, pretending to be afraid, and then wrapped his sinewy arms around me and buried his head in my neck. "But my *Boy* will save me," he said in my ear. "My *Boy* will say, 'I love one African man. Let him live!'" He kissed me on the ear and whispered, "N'est-ce pas?"

Then one day I received a letter from Jessie Ray informing me that she and Dean were coming to Dakar to spend Christmas with me. Enclosed was a package of letters written by ten-year-old girls in the First Baptist Church, commending me for my work as a missionary in Africa.

I read the letters as I sat on my windowsill, with one leg dangling over the side of the building and a fifth of Four Roses bourbon beside me. In the parking lot, seven stories down, the guard turned his wrinkled face up and squinted. To Muslims, bare legs are more provocative than bare breasts. I waved and poured more bourbon into my Coke. I unfolded the letter again and imagined that it read, "It is with great sadness that I inform you that your mother and father were not among the survivors of this plane crash . . ."

I had not told my parents that I had a Senegalese lover, and I had not told Yousouf that I had parents. "Merde!" I said to the empty room. Then I staggered to my feet, took a mask off the wall, and fitted it over my face. I stood in front of the mirror and practiced explaining to Yousouf, in French, the sudden appearance of a woman and a man I called Mom and Dad.

The right moment to give this speech never arose. I ended up blurting out my confession in bed, two days before my parents' arrival.

"Tu rêves," Yousouf mumbled, pulling the blanket back over his head. He shivered in the seventy-degree winters, and since I insisted on keeping the windows open, this was how he slept.

"I'm not dreaming." I pulled the cover away from his face. His hair was cut short, and his ears were small and round, fitted close to his head. I traced them with my finger. "My parents are coming on Christmas Eve. You have to move your clothes out of my closet."

He sat up, crossed his arms over his chest, and shivered. "On ne t'a pas trouvé dans une poubelle?"

I winced. "No, I wasn't found in a trash can. I lied."

"Donc, tu n'es pas orpheline?" I would miss the sound of that word. Who could help but love someone called *orpheline?*

I took a gulp from the wineglass on my nightstand and said, "No. I'm not an orphan. I'm just an asshole."

"What's an asshole?"

I pointed to my rear end. He raised his eyebrows and carefully repeated the word. When I stood up to refill my glass, he said, "Bring me a mango juice, asshole."

When I got back into bed, Yousouf said, "You know, Darren, in Africa we say that if there are two paths, and on the shorter path there is a man who waits to kill you, then it is faster to take the longer path. I am surprised that now you tell me you are not an *orpheline,* but I am not angry. To Americans words seem very important, but in Senegal the words are not the meaning."

Then, apparently remembering that I had told him he was supposed to hug me when I cried, he put one arm awkwardly around me and patted my head. "You drink too much," he said. "You are young and pretty and intelligent. You have a man who doesn't drink, and now you have parents. Why are you wanting to die?"

"I want to live," I said. "I just have too many lives."

"You are too complicated, Darren. I know you do not like my advices, but listen to me this one thing. When your parents come here, show them our African hospitality. Show them *teranga.*" I stared out the window. "Boy. Sss, Boy-bi." He caught my chin in his hand and turned my face toward his. Then he rapped his knuckles lightly on my head, as though testing its hardness, and said, "Têtue." Our child, he had told me, would be beautiful and stubborn.

The next night Yousouf packed up his toothbrush, razor, and shaving cream and took all of his suits out of my closet. "My mother is not concerned about your color," he told me as he examined my pink polo shirt and then added it to his suitcase. "But she asks me not to live with you, and she says I should not marry you except on the condition that you convert to Islam. I answer her that the American girl is too independent. N'est-ce pas?"

"That's my shirt," I said.

"Our shirt. Why do you put your parents to a hotel? They should sleep here in your bed. You can sleep on the floor. You should not drink all the time alone in your apartment. It is Jessie

Ray and Dean who are the orphans." He paused in front of the mirror to pat his hair smooth. "Hello, Mr. Parkman," he said, holding his hand out to the glass and smiling. "Hello, Papa."

On Christmas Eve, he drove me to the airport and waited in the car while I went inside to find my parents. I was half the size of the average gazelle-legged Senegalese, and I used this to my advantage. I bent low as I sped through the crowd, clasping my purse to my belly and sticking my elbows out.

"Mademoiselle!" hissed a boy. He sidled up beside me and spread his long black fingers across my arm. "Mademoiselle, attends!" I ducked and turned, slick as a greased ball in water.

I spotted Dean and Jessie Ray before they got through the gates. They were wearing London Fog trench coats and stood next to a pile of matching leather luggage. Their cheeks were pink with excitement and, like all Americans in foreign countries, they looked absurdly friendly. I waved. They looked right through me.

Dean walked away from Jessie Ray and stared intently into the crowd of black bodies around me. He wore a tweed cap. Beneath his open trench coat he wore starched, creased khaki pants, a V-neck sweater the color of corn silk, and a blue button-down shirt. He had replaced his gold watch with a plastic one, as I had instructed in my last letter, but neither he nor Jessie Ray had followed my suggestion to remove their wedding rings.

"Dad!" I called, waving my arm. "Dad, I'm here!" He looked frantically all around me.

When he saw me, his eyes glowed, and his arm shot into the air and stayed there, waving. "Darren!" he cried. "Hi, Darren!" There was a huge, silly grin on his face, and he kept waving. Tears rolled out of my eyes and I tried to squeeze them back.

Still waving, he called out, "Jessie Ray!" The Tennessee accent reverberated through the airport, and people stared at him. "She's over here! I found her! Here she is!"

Jessie Ray spun around. For a moment she tossed her head this way and that, and then she threw her arm up in a wave. She had once held the title of Miss Western Tennessee and she still walked as though she wore a banner across her chest. She had never learned how to smile, but her eyes shone with soft lights. They were sea green, shadowed with an intelligence that would have been unnerving if one could stare into them longer than the second she permitted.

"Now hold on to your bags," I said as I led them outside. "Watch your rings. These guys will pull them right off your fingers."

"Bàyyileen suma yaay!" I yelled to the two boys leaning in close to Jessie Ray.

In greasy English, one of them was saying, "Madame! Hello, Madame. Are you from Los Angeles, California?"

"Hello," she said. "No, we're from Stipple —" One of the boys was already untying her shoelace so she would look down while the other one went for her pocket.

"Thief!" I shouted. "Get lost!" A man pulled on Dean's suitcase, crying, "Taxi! Venez, Monsieur!" Dean pulled back on the handle, smiling all around with his Rotary Club smile. "This must be the welcoming committee," he said. A leper planted himself in front of him and rattled a coffee can of coins.

"Aycaleen!" I yelled. As I looked for Yousouf's car, I waved my hands at the tightening circle around us.

"Why are they hissing?" asked Jessie Ray. "I don't know why I minored in French. I don't remember a word of it." To the delight of the crowd, she hissed back. "They sure are black," she said, as a man pushed an African mask in her face. "And tall."

Suddenly a boy scooted into our circle on a homemade skate-board. He had no legs and rode the board on his belly, propelling himself with both hands, on which he wore flip-flops. He wheeled right up to Jessie Ray, raised himself off the board with his hands, and said, "Bonjour, Madame." He smiled. "Donne-moi cent francs."

"Lord-a-mercy," said Jessie Ray. "Dean, look at this one."

"Ba beneen yoon," I said to the boy. "Tomorrow." He paddled around with his hands and turned his sly face up to me. "Oh, you speak Wolof," he said in French. "May ma xaalis." His voice was unctuous, wheedling, and hard as the cement beneath his hands. When I didn't give him the money, he demanded it in French.

"I told you to go away." I turned my back to him and looked for Yousouf.

"You told me to go away?" he repeated, as though amazed by my rudeness. "I beg your pardon, Mademoiselle. I'm not talking to you anyway."

When he wheeled around to Dean, I jumped between them. "Aycaleen, demleen!" I shouted. "Bàyyil suma Pàpp! Bàyyil suma yaay!" I yelled this so harshly that my voice broke. I waved my arms at all of them, rasping, "You're rude! You're not normal!"

"Nous sommes corrects!" the legless boy yelled back. "You're the one who is rude!" The smooth mask of charm had dropped from his face. He laughed in a long hiss and called me a whore.

"Go to hell!" I screamed. I wanted to kick his head and send him flopping off the sidewalk.

My parents were watching me with wide eyes. "Why Darren," said Jessie Ray, "I believe you're acting uglier than they are."

Then Yousouf hopped out of his car, parting the crowd as he walked up to greet us. Dean gave him the same noncommittal smile he was giving all the black men around him and pulled back on the suitcase. "Dad!" I said in a low voice. "This is my friend. This is Yousouf. He wants to put your suitcase in the car."

Yousouf smiled. He looked sharp in his suit, a navy blue one that he wore with my pink polo shirt and the tie I had given him last Christmas.

"Excuse me," said Dean. He released the suitcase to shake Yousouf's hand. He had told me once that he judged a man by his fingernails. As I watched the white hand clasp the black one, I checked Yousouf's manicure; it was perfect. "Don jour," Dean said.

Without a second's hesitation, Yousouf replied, "Bonjour, Monsieur." In English he said, "You have only been in Senegal for half an hour, and you are already speaking French."

"Just one word of it," said Dean, following him to the car.

"It's *bond jour,* Dean," said Jessie Ray, "not *don jour.* B as in 'boy.'"

"You sit in the back seat with your parents," said Yousouf. In the car, Dean patted my knee and beamed at me. "It's been seven hundred and nineteen days since I last saw you," he said. "I counted each one."

"What beautiful weather," said Jessie Ray. "It's just like Hawaii." On Avenue Pompidou, they laughed at the giant black Santa Claus revolving on a rooftop.

"I guess the Africans would think Santa Claus is black," said Dean. "I never thought of that."

"Don't be prejudiced, Dean."

"That wasn't prejudiced. I just said —"

"We didn't think the Muslims celebrated Christmas," Jessie Ray said. "We brought you a tape of Christmas carols and a Christmas tree, a miniature one with miniature lights and ornaments and even miniature tinsel."

"I plugged the lights in to make sure they work," said Dean.

Each time he spoke to me, he touched me, as though he feared I wasn't really there. They thanked Yousouf for carrying the luggage up to the apartment but barely noticed when he left.

Still wearing her trench coat, Jessie Ray stood in the center of my living room and said, "Darren, I have missed you. You may not think so." Her nose turned red, the way it did when she was going to cry.

"Hug your mother's neck," said Dean. "She loves you." I gave her a bear hug.

"Your dad missed you," said Jessie Ray, digging in her black pocketbook for a Kleenex. "Went through a depression. Just sat in that chair every night. Moped. Sometimes he'd go in your room and just stand there. I got to where I had to leave the house."

When we looked at him, Dean smiled bashfully. He was sitting on the vinyl couch where no one ever sat. "This couch must have a loose screw in it somewhere," he said. He bounced twice in his seat and then got down on his knees to look beneath the frame.

Dean's hair was completely white, and his pink scalp showed through the strands he combed over his bald spot. Jessie Ray's hair was a color she called bronze. She wore a red dress covered with lions and zebras and a chunky necklace she had bought in Memphis. Both of them looked so white.

"Here," said Jessie Ray. "I brought some of my work to show you. I'm doing African art now." She rummaged through a suitcase and handed me a sheaf of prints she had made with cut potatoes and ink. As I flipped through the primitive images of lions, tigers, and turtles, she said, "My art teacher thinks I should change my name. Jessie Ray doesn't sound like an artist's name. She suggested I use my maiden name — Darren — but I told her that was your name now. You wouldn't like that, would you?"

When I didn't raise my head, she said, "I didn't think so. Do you want one of these prints? They're not very good. The potatoes were a little soft." I took the turtle and studied her signature in the corner.

"I like your name," I said.

"It's country. Everybody had a double name back then. We didn't have much, but we got two names."

Through the open windows, the sound of drums beat into the room.

"The natives are getting restless," said Dean.

"It's probably a wrestling match," I said.

"Your apartment sure is clean." He gave the couch two shakes, dusted the wooden frame off with his handkerchief, and then walked to the window.

"It's bare," said Jessie Ray, "but she likes it that way. Spartan."

Yousouf and I had recently redecorated the apartment. After we hung the black curtains figured with white fish skeletons, he had said, "This is our home." Then he pulled out his key, winking at me before he slipped it back into his pocket.

"So this is your color scheme," said Jessie Ray. "Black and white."

"Is Use-off one of your students at the university?" asked Dean.

"He said he works at a bank," said Jessie Ray. "You don't listen."

"He's a real good-natured fellow."

"He's a good-looking boy," said Jessie Ray. "Cute personality."

Dean tested the window on its hinge until he was satisfied that it didn't need oiling. Then he looked out. "You've got an ocean view," he said. "This is good real estate property. I thought you'd be living like a pauper over here in Africa. Does the Peace Corps pay the rent?"

"The Senegalese government stole it for me."

"We've got to get that sunset," said Jessie Ray. She set up the camcorder, but the light wouldn't come on. Long after the sun had dropped into the sea, she and Dean were still arguing.

"Well, dad-blame it then; you read the directions yourself," she said. She handed him her owl-eyed glasses, which he set firmly on his face. Then he opened the instruction booklet and snapped the pages between his fingers.

"It's all in Japanese," he said.

I suspected that the print was just too small for him to read, but I said, "How silly of them to write in their own language."

"She's getting crabby," said Jessie Ray. "We should go to our hotel and let her rest." As we walked out the door, she glanced at the pack of Marlboros in my hand and said, "Still smoking, I see. I brought you a picture of a black lung."

"That was thoughtful of you," I said. Then I felt mean. I put my arms around her rigid back and dropped my head on her shoulder.

She gave me a quick hug and pushed me away, saying, "I just don't want to go to your funeral. Children should outlive their parents."

"I don't guess this place would burn down to the quick," said Dean, "with all this cement." He watched me lock the door and waited until I had stepped away from it before he tried the handle to make sure it was locked.

"There's no fire escape," said Jessie Ray. "Don't take the elevator if there's a fire."

Dean stopped. "Goodness gracious no!" He looked hard at me. I was trying to untie my goatskin bag to get some matches. "I can never untie your knots, Dad. Why did you tie my bag?"

"I was trying to help you. I didn't want everything to fall out. Here, I'll get it. Don't ever get in the elevator if there's a fire."

"I know that."

"She knows that," said Jessie Ray.

"She's a smart girl." He patted me on the back. "I guess she'd get out pretty quick." As the gray walls of the elevator closed around us, he said, "I guess they don't have fire drills in Africa."

As I walked them down the street to their hotel I held their hands. "Don't go outside," I said. "Don't talk to anyone. I'll be here in the morning to get you."

"Now you know what we went through when you were a kid," said Jessie Ray. "Every time I turned my back, you had wandered off somewhere." I had already decided that if they showed up at my apartment during the night, Yousouf would have to crawl out the window and stand on the ledge. Since he was afraid of heights, I didn't know how I would get him out there, but I intended to try.

When I got back to my apartment I found Yousouf in bed with the Ziploc bag of brownies Jessie Ray had brought me. He was trying to sing along with "Frosty the Snowman." The lights of the Christmas tree scattered like sequins over his black arms. "C'est cool, ça," he said, examining the zipper of the bag. "These clever Americans."

I stretched out beside him with a glass of bourbon. "Do white people look funny to you?"

"Toubab." He drew out the word the way children did on street corners and tossed my hair with his hands, saying, "*Toubab* hair! Ha, ha." Then he was serious. "Your family is handsome. Dean and Jessie Ray seem wise. Ils sont *nice*, quoi." As he ran his hand along my thigh, I watched the colored lights of the Christmas tree slide over our skins. "Eh, orpheline?" I pressed my face into his shoulder, and he took the glass out of my hand, saying softly, "Suma Boy, kooku daal," a phrase from a song about a woman leaving a man.

On Christmas day, at 9:00 A.M. sharp, I sat Jessie Ray and Dean on the rickety wooden bench beside the parking lot of my building. This gave Yousouf some extra time to get out of the apartment.

"Now make sure you don't leave your pick on the sink," I had told him, "or a sock on the floor, or your —" I stopped. I sounded exactly like Dean and Jessie Ray.

"I am going to lean out the window and yell, 'Hello, Papa Dean! Hello, Mama Jessie Ray!'" Yousouf said. He took my chin in his hand and kissed me.

After dark, the whores did their business in a thin strip of trees along the edge of the street, but in the morning the area belonged to a bent little man in a red stocking cap who sold coffee and bread. "They served a breakfast buffet at the hotel," said Jessie Ray, narrowing her eyes as the man rinsed out a dirty plastic cup and began stirring Nescafé and hot water into it. "Are we drinking after people?"

We opened gifts in my apartment. Islamic chants screamed out of the mosque's loudspeakers in a static roar, drowning out Handel's *Messiah*. As Dean unwrapped the grinning wooden mask rolled in one of my old curtains — yellow *lagos* printed with squiggly violet creatures — he said, "This will be yours someday. You'll inherit all of the African things."

"She won't inherit everything," said Jessie Ray. "The other children will get their share, too."

"She'll inherit all the African things. These are hers."

"Stop talking about dying," I said. I checked my watch to see if it was too early for a drink. It was midmorning.

"Open another present," said Dean. He had a smile on his face, and with his eyes he was telling me to smile now. I tore the red paper from the package and removed the polo shirts I had already planned to rewrap and give to Yousouf after my parents went home.

"These are going to swallow you whole," said Jessie Ray, "but I got the size you wanted. I guess you like them big." As I set the shirts on top of the heap of other gifts, I considered telling them the truth, but Dean was still trying to make me smile, and Jessie Ray had taken out her camera.

I wanted to take my parents to a Catholic monastery where Senegalese drums were played during the service, but Jessie Ray insisted on going to the Baptist mission. She had contacted the missionaries from Tennessee.

"Most of the Senegalese are devout Muslims," I said. "The rest are devout Catholics or devout animists. Do you know how many converts the Baptists have snatched up in the last five years?"

"I don't care for your language," said Jessie Ray.

"Two," I said. "And those were Methodists from Sierra Leone."

"Ha, ha," said Dean. "Everybody get along."

The service was terrible. It was centered around a duet performed by the missionary couple's two daughters — lanky girls with stringy blonde hair and pink combs sticking out of their back pockets. Neither of them could sing a note. One of them forgot the words. I rolled my eyes at Jessie Ray, who stared straight ahead and pretended not to notice.

Afterward, she cornered the preacher and made a big deal about how we were all Americans here in Senegal and all Baptist to the bone. "How many people in your fellowship are Senegalese?" she asked, glancing at me to make sure I was listening.

"Well," he drawled, "I don't know. They all look alike to me."

"Darren can tell them apart," said Jessie Ray.

When we were back in the taxi she said, "You're right. He was a dumbbell." Then she leaned out of the window with the camcorder and shot everything on the street, which I had asked her not to do. Someone threw a rock at the taxi.

Later that night when I heard Yousouf's knock on my door — two long raps and a short one — I stayed in the window. I wanted to know if he would use his key. When I heard his footsteps moving away, I ran to the door and opened it.

He stood very straight in the doorway and kept his arms by his sides. "Qu'est-ce qu'il y a, Darren?"

"Don't leave me, Yousouf. Please don't leave me."

"My *Boy.* You feel solitary." Then he saw the bottle in the window. He frowned. Loosening his tie, he walked to the bedroom, saying, "Really, you are difficult sometimes. I want to use the key, because I am thinking, maybe she is sitting in the window drinking bourbon and will fall. Then I am thinking, maybe Dean and Jessie Ray are here. They will ask, 'Why does this boy have a key?'" He sat down on the edge of our bed and removed his socks and shoes. Without looking at me, he shined each shoe with a sock and set the pair neatly against the wall. "You see, Darren, the pains you give me."

"Why do I have to pretend that you're just my friend? The man I love is none of my parents' business. They can't run my life."

He was silent as he undressed and hung his clothes in my closet. Naked, he lay down and folded his arms behind his head. "You must respect your parents. I notice that you do not do this enough." As I climbed in beside him, he pulled me against his chest and drew the sheet over our heads. His smooth, supple skin smelled of indigo. I tightened my arms around him and licked the silky hollow in his neck.

"What afraids you, Darren?"

"Nothing."

"But there are many things to be afraid of in Africa. Three o'clock in the morning is the worst time. Then you can see a white horse, or even a woman. You know, if you see a white woman at this hour, she is the devil. She will make you make love to her, and then you will be schizophrenic."

Long ago I had stopped trying to convince Yousouf that there was no such thing as magic. Like most black Muslims in Senegal, he ranked witch doctors with religious men and insisted that genies were mentioned throughout the Koran.

"What scares you?" I asked, expecting another horror story about the *kangkurang,* a spirit dressed up as a tree that chased newly circumcised boys, or the genies that come through open windows at night and jump inside your chest to eat your heart.

"I am afraid that you will go back to the United States and forget me here." When he kissed me his face was wet.

In the middle of the night I woke up to the crack of bone against bone. Outside, under the low curse of a man, a whore wailed. Yousouf was leaning out of the window. The faint light from the streetlamps exposed the delicate ribs moving beneath his skin and cast a purple sheen on his smooth, round buttocks. Somewhere in the trees the whore laughed, then sobbed, then laughed again, high and wild. Again the man hit her, and again she screamed.

"Stop him," I said, sitting up in bed. "Do something!" When he didn't answer, I thought he might have walked in his sleep. I ran to the window and screamed, "Leave her alone, you black son of a bitch!"

"Viens, toi!" Yousouf pulled me away from the window.

"Why is she here? Why doesn't she leave him?"

"She is a whore," he said, holding my wrists. "She has no mother. Where would she go?"

"I'm sorry. Yousouf, I'm sorry I said that."

"You have stress. This is very obvious." For a moment it was so quiet outside that we could hear the ocean washing up on the sand. Beyond the streetlamps, all around the city, drums beat in and out like the heart of a beast holding Dakar against its chest.

The next morning Jessie Ray came to my apartment. Yousouf had left ten minutes earlier to hire a taxi to take us to his mother's village. When I saw Jessie Ray standing at the door my heart jumped and then my head began to hurt. "What's wrong?" I demanded.

"Nothing is wrong. You look tired. Did you stay up late? Dean is coming. He wanted to take the stairs. He's all in a dither because there's not a fire escape in your building."

"I told y'all not to leave the hotel without me." I glanced around the room to make sure Yousouf hadn't left anything lying about. To me, the whole apartment smelled like sex. "Last week a seventy-year-old Peace Corps volunteer was beaten up and mugged in broad daylight. I don't know why you won't listen to me."

"We're not seventy yet," she said. "Two fellows did follow us real close, trying to sell us some watches, but I told them we weren't interested. They snickered about it but didn't bother us after that. I'd like some coffee."

I followed her into the kitchen, where she put a pan of water on the stove and found the Nescafé. I leaned against the sink, blocking it from her view, but Yousouf had already washed and dried our two coffee cups and put them away.

"I don't know how you live without hot water," she said. "I guess you've got some things to look forward to when you come back home." She made a face as she sipped her instant coffee and then said, "So you want a white house with a picket fence and a German shepherd. No husband?" I had written about the house and dog in a letter. "No grandchildren?"

"You'll have grandpups."

"Thank you." She straightened her vest. "I got this out of your closet at home," she said. "I hope you don't mind. You left it."

"It looks nice on you." It was a fringed suede vest embroidered with cowgirls; I had worn it when I was sixteen.

"I can still wear young clothes," she said. "Whenever I show my senior citizen discount card at the grocery store, the cashiers can't believe that I'm sixty." As she twisted the towel in her veined hand I watched the diamond glint on her finger. Dean had given her the ring when she was twenty-one, and she had never removed it.

Now she looked around my kitchen as if she might find a machine gun leaning against the wall, or a black man peering out from a cabinet. I knew that she had made this unannounced visit to see what I was really doing in Senegal, and in a way I admired her for that. Jessie Ray was tough.

"More coffee?" I asked.

She cleared her throat and said, "You aren't planning to marry Yousouf, I hope."

"He's just a friend."

"You better make that clear to him. He sure does seem to like you."

"I'll keep us white."

"It's not that. Yousouf is a good-looking man, and just as nice as he can be, but there are cultural differences that you should be aware of. Religious differences. A man is so different from a woman to begin with that you don't want to start out with somebody as different as a . . . Martian."

I brushed past her, took a beer out of the refrigerator, opened it with my army knife, and drank. She stared. "I have a headache," I said.

"Louise Darren Parkman." When she pressed her lips together, the wrinkles around her mouth cut into deep lines. The rest of her face seemed to sag. "Why do you need alcohol at eight o'clock in the morning?"

"My head hurts." For a split second she looked me in the eye. Then she turned away. I finished the beer in silence while she looked for an aspirin.

In the parking lot, while the driver tied our luggage on the roof of his taxi, Dean explained our change of plans to Jessie Ray.

"Yousouf's father is spending the holidays with his third wife here in Dakar, so Yousouf is lending his car to them." He spoke as though he had been dealing with the nuisances of polygamy all of his life. "We're going to take a taxi to the village. Yousouf's mother is the first wife." If Yousouf drove his Peugeot into the village he would be hounded for money the rest of his life.

"Where's the taxi?" asked Jessie Ray.

"This is it," said Dean, pointing to the blue and yellow van painted with pictures of African women carrying bowls of fruit on their heads, African men dancing around them, palm trees, and big yellow suns. One window was covered with cardboard, and the front window appeared to have been put back in with tape. Across the back of the van, in heavy black letters, there were supplications to Allah.

The driver was arguing with Yousouf about the price. Apparently he had thought Yousouf would be traveling with Africans, and now that he saw the leather luggage and the cameras, he insisted that we all pay the *toubab* price.

"Déedéet!" said Yousouf. He pressed his hand to his breast and flapped his arm like a chicken wing, twice, to emphasize his refusal. Each time the driver pulled a bag off the roof, Yousouf returned it. "You can board," he told me. I jerked open the door, which almost came off the hinges, and held it for Jessie Ray.

"Put the camera away and get in the car," I said. "Please, Mom. Don't take the driver's picture. It's not polite. He isn't an animal in a zoo."

"Yousouf lets us take his picture," she said. She climbed in the car and made a face through the cracked window. "What I can't understand is how you can tell us that we are being impolite when you are so rude to your parents."

After we were all in the van the driver cursed, jumped in his seat, and jammed a piece of wire into the ignition. The prayer beads and the blonde kewpie doll hanging from his rearview mirror swung against each other as we bounced down the road. He drove like Evel Knievel, slamming around cars that had stopped for lights, bearing down on goats crossing the road, skidding to stops in front of children. Once, for no apparent reason, he drove down a street in reverse.

"I'm just not going to look," said Jessie Ray, widening her eyes as another van, top-heavy with rams, careened toward us. Then we were out of the city and the desert stretched out on both sides of the road, vast and empty.

The taxi dropped us off at a *marché*, where we piled onto a donkey cart driven by a gaunt man with dust in his hair. He lashed a whip across the donkey's ribs and we bumped down a rutted path into the dry millet fields. The millet was just stubble poking up through the sand. There was nothing else on the ground but enormous anthills.

"We've got to get pictures of these," said Dean. Yousouf told the driver to stop, and Dean and Jessie Ray got out with the camcorder and two hand-held cameras, one for slides and one for prints, to photograph the anthills. While the donkey nosed around in the sand for something to eat, the driver cleaned his teeth with a chew stick.

"Why are they looking at those?" he asked Yousouf. It was as odd as if an African had been riding through New York City in a taxi and had asked to stop so he could photograph the fire hydrants.

As the sun rose higher in the sky, my eyes began to hurt behind my sunglasses. There was nothing between us and the sun — no building, no tree, no cloud. The sky was a white glow. It would have been easy to see pools of blue water in the distance, but there were none. There was nothing around us but dirt and light. "Imagine living way out here without a car," said Dean. "What if you needed a doctor?"

An hour later we came to a circle of mud huts that looked like forts children might build. The tin roofs shimmered like water. A woman with a baby strapped to her back stood over the well, rapidly throwing one hand over the other as she drew up a leaking bag of water. Nearby, a girl pounded millet with a pestle as long as an oar. She sang, threw the pestle up in the air, and clapped her hands twice before she caught it. Her arms were beautifully toned.

The children had seen us coming and were running toward us. They wore ragged clothes donated by the Salvation Army and their bellies were swollen up like balloons.

"Jëre-jëf waay," I said to the driver as I reached into my purse for the fare.

"I'll pay for it," said Dean.

"Don't open your wallet. You have more C.F.A. in your pocket than the average Senegalese man makes in a year."

He put his arm around my shoulder and said, "You're going to make it." The love in his eyes embarrassed me. I didn't know where to look, so I reworked the latch on my purse. "I was worried about leaving you alone when I die. I can't leave this earth without knowing that you're all situated. You've grown up out here, though. I think you can fend for yourself now. That gives me peace of mind."

"All she needs is money," said Jessie Ray. Before we were even out of the cart, she had the camera rolling. The children halted a short distance away from us and bunched together, giggling and falling against each other as they called out, "Toubab! Toubab! Toubab!"

"What are they saying?" asked Dean.

"Honky."

"Play ball!" cried Jessie Ray. She hastily tore the Christmas paper from a red rubber ball and threw it to them. Shrieking, they began to fight for it. In a robotic voice, she said into the camcorder, "We are now in Yousouf's village. Yousouf is Darren's friend in Senegal, West Africa. He is working on his Ph.D. in economics and works for the present time at a bank. These are the village children." Then she handed the camera to Dean and ran into the crowd, clapping her hands and crying, "Ball! Throw the ball!"

The men, who had risen from their mats to greet us, didn't know what to make of this spectacle. "Please, Mom," I said with my teeth clenched. "Please pay attention. We're supposed to greet the village elders. This is rude. You're embarrassing me."

"Oh, hush," said Jessie Ray. She threw the ball back into the crowd of screaming children, crying, "Whee! Whee! Play ball!" An old man wearing a ragged brown robe and a fake leopard-skin cape looked at my mother in amazement. "Kii borom kër la," said Yousouf, and he went to greet the head of the village.

"Dad," I said. "The chief is staring at Mom. Make her behave." He put his arm around me. "She's just excited," he said. "We've never been in a village before. Show me what you want me to do."

We shook hands, first with the men, then with the women who stood behind them retying their *pagnes* around their waists, and finally with the children, who were rounded up by a woman who switched their ankles with a stick. They edged shyly toward us and held out their limp hands.

I studied all of the women's faces, looking for Yousouf's mother, whom I had never met. At last she emerged from a dark doorway in a billowing white cloud of gauze. Instantly I recognized Yousouf's face. On her the jaw was softer and the cheekbones were not quite as sharp, but those were his eyes.

Her upper lip was painted a deep red and her gums were dyed

blue. Gold earrings glinted from her ears. She was a big woman but she curtsied nimbly before Dean. When he curtsied back, the other women laughed.

Dean enjoyed the attention. He glanced away from a buxom young woman in a black bra who couldn't stop giggling, and held his hand out to Yousouf's mother. "Dean Parkman," he said loudly. "Don jour."

She looked just to the side of his head, which was level with her own, and said, "Bonjour, Monsieur." This was the extent of her French. Yousouf translated our greetings. When he introduced me to her, she looked me dead in the eye.

I had asked Yousouf once how she felt when his father married a second wife.

"My mother is a good Muslim," he said. "She turned to the education of the children. She gave to us all of her love."

"Did she love your father?" I asked.

"Very much. I used to hear them laughing in bed. They were in love. But she got old. She had her children, and we still needed her."

Now she looked about forty. Her face was smooth and glossy, but I could see the years in her eyes.

She spoke in Mandinka, a soft language from the jungles of the Casamance, as indecipherable as the sound of rain. As she talked, she continued to look me in the eye. The sun burned down on us, and flies gathered around my eyes and mouth and nose. I let them land without trying to brush them away — she stood so still. I tried to show my respect by glancing away now and then, but I wanted to see everything in her eyes. She was the most serene person I had ever met. Finally, she finished speaking and was silent.

Yousouf turned his head to look at Jessie Ray, who had picked up a naked baby with talismans tied around its neck and belly. Then he looked down at Dean's white loafers and translated,

"My mother says that since she does not speak French or Wolof, and you do not speak Mandinka, you cannot talk to each other." She smiled at me. There was nothing coy or malicious in it. It was a beautiful smile, kind and wise, and I understood that she would never give me her son.

"I'm her mother," said Jessie Ray, stepping in front of me to shake her hand. "Mmotherrr," she said loudly, stretching her lips to exaggerate each syllable. The fringe on her vest swung as she turned to point at me and back to herself. The sun bore down on us with the hot white intensity of a spotlight. When I began to see red, I closed my eyes.

With my nostrils full of the smell of sweat and milk and dung, I looked past the shifting red dots behind my eyelids and saw myself in America, laying flowers on my parents' graves and walking back to a white picket fence, through the gate, past a German shepherd, and into my house.

"Darren," said Yousouf. "Ça va?"

"Ça va," I replied, opening my eyes.

NDANK, NDANK

When I told Yousouf that I needed to change my life, he said I should fire Rokhaya and employ a maid who knew her place. Rokhaya disagreed. She suggested that I drop Yousouf and try to catch a white man. If a Caucasian male visited me, Rokhaya hardly let him get all the way out the door before she said in Wolof, "He loves you." She would touch her finger to her eye to show me that she was not blind. "He loves Darren," she said. "Góorgi bëgg na Darren. This man wants Darren."

"Waaw." I would bob my head, yawn. I had lived in Dakar for over two years and I was jaded. I needed something bigger than a man, bigger even than my bartender, Awa, whose butt swelled out like a wave when she walked and who could read minds.

"You need to lay off the booze," the Peace Corps doctor had told me.

"How?" I asked him. He looked at me through his gold

spectacles while I tried not to squirm in my chair. "Drink Coke," he said. "Drink Goldens. Drink water."

"For how long?"

He wouldn't say. Every week I went in for a sobriety check. When he asked me how I was doing on the wagon, I said, "Fine." Sometimes I had to sit on my hands to keep them from shaking. Our talks were so disturbing that afterward I always jumped in a taxi and went straight to Awa's bar.

"Oh happy day!" the bouncer said when he opened the door for me. Tonton's English was limited to lines from the '70s hits on Awa's jukebox, and he tended to sing the words. He was the wrestling champion of Senegal and no more necessary to the bar at L'Hotel Rouge than I was, but Awa always employed her lovers so she could keep an eye on them.

It was Awa who suggested that I needed magic. When I told Yousouf that I intended to get a *gris-gris* to make me stop drinking, he became angry.

"The *gris-gris* are not toys," he said, staring me down. "These are not souvenirs for you to take back to the United States. The *marabout* is a man of God. How can you ask for a gift from a man of God when you yourself are an atheist? This is what questions me."

"Maybe I have a god," I said.

"Ha! This is your god." When he motioned his elbow toward the beer in my hand, I tightened my grip on the green bottle.

Yousouf put up with me until the night I went skinny-dipping in the indoor pool that was separated by a glass wall from Awa's bar at L'Hotel Rouge. I don't remember anything that happened that night, but when I got up the next morning I found a note on the bathroom sink. It read:

You shame me. I try to do some good for you and even speak English and wash dishes which I have never done for another woman, but you treat me without respect. It is too hard. I am leaving you until the end of time with the exception of coming to take my clothes and music away. Excuse me, but I am not loving you.

Au revoir,

Yousouf

I looked in the mirror. The night before I had broken every heart in the bar, but this morning I looked like something the cat spit up. I discovered a wrinkle and hurriedly dabbed it with cream, hoping it wasn't permanent. After I ran a comb through my hair and brushed my teeth, I got down on my hands and knees and began to vomit into the toilet.

I spent the day in bed with slices of cucumber over my eyes, pretending I was buried in a nice cool coffin, but my head pounded, my stomach churned, and I couldn't quench my thirst. Worst of all, I couldn't stop thinking.

At exactly five o'clock I allowed myself a cocktail. Tonton's Land Rover squealed into the parking lot. A moment later, Awa emerged in a flowing *boubou* made of orange gauze and trimmed with gold braid. I slid to the floor and hid behind the black curtains as she called out, "Oh, sweetness, where are you?"

My apartment was on the seventh floor, but her voice carried into the room as clearly as if she were in the kitchen. "Sweetness, look out the window. Your chariot has arrived." I sat so still that my feet went to sleep, but I knew that Awa had seen me, so I stuck my head out the window. "There you are!" she sang out. "Were you balking? How often do chariots arrive at your door, that you may dig your little heels in the sand and balk?"

"Come on up."

"Pardon?" When she raised her arms, the sleeves swept up like wings. "You are not asking me to walk up those stairs. Do I look like a goat to you? Where are your glasses, sweetness? Do you

not see, standing below you, a fat, middle-aged woman? Surely
you are not asking a fat, middle-aged woman to walk up seven
flights of stairs. No, surely not."

Take the elevator, I thought.

"And surely," she said in the same singsong voice, "you would
not be so foolish as to ask this fat old woman to place her person
in that tin coffin you so proudly refer to as your elevator? How
can you carry on like this when there is a chariot waiting for
you?"

I threw on some clothes and went down. When she saw me
trudging across the courtyard, she put her hands on her hips and
began to shake her head back and forth. "As if every day a
chariot arrives at your door to take you on an adventure," she
said. "Look at you! Is that a frown on your baby face?"

"Where are we going?"

"I have come to your rescue, and you stand here in your
Brownie suit, balking. Really, you are shocking. Tonton has kept
the engine running; we're putting you in the back."

"Hello, darlin'," said Tonton as I crawled in the back of the
Land Rover. "Na nga def?" He twisted around in the seat to
smile at me.

"Maa ngi fii rekk," I said. "I'm here only. Lan la?" I stuck the
tip of my tongue out of the corner of my mouth, a polite way of
pointing, to indicate the writhing sack next to me. Tonton laughed
and, blaring the horn, spun the jeep out into the road.

"Ganaar la rekk!"

"I thought to provide the sacrificial rooster," said Awa. "We
are taking you to Conté the *Conja* man, if you remember."

"Total blank." I untied the Gold Coast Rambler scarf from
around my neck and tied it around my head so I wouldn't look
like a Brownie. I lit a cigarette and tried not to look at the sack,
which gave me the creeps, even when it was still.

"Don't tell me that you have already forgotten your performance last night. You went straight to the diving board, removed your clothing, and did a belly flop. Half of all the eligible men in Dakar, plus the ineligible ones, stood with their noses pressed against the glass wall, watching you."

This was only the second blackout I'd had in my life, but I'd been in a brownout for years. I'd developed a vague smile, learned to laugh at myself, and come to expect surprises. On good days I was a merry visitor from another planet; on bad days I considered myself a scientist. I wanted to explain this to Awa, but my head hurt and my mouth felt like someone had stuffed it with a rag.

"Yousouf left me," I said.

She turned around. Up close, her face was not beautiful. She was half Sierra-Leonian, half New Yorker, and her skin was the color of the Chattahoochee River. Her nose and mouth were large and seemed to have been borrowed from some plain, practical person. One glass eye reflected light, and one real eye saw down to the bottom of my soul.

"No!" she cried. "Not the handsome Yousouf Tall you've been threatening to marry? Have you worried your dear parents and created a revolution in Tennessee for nothing? I liked him. He had such a wonderful jaw. What did you do to that poor boy, Darren? He was madly in love with you."

"Lan la?" asked Tonton, and Awa quickly translated the situation into French.

"C'est dommage!" He looked appropriately stricken. Then he quickly assured me in French that my boyfriend would come back because I was pretty, and American women were hard to get. In English he sang, "American woman!" and laughed.

"Shit happens."

"Sweetness, if I am not mistaken, this boy was smitten."

"Seriñ bi, fumu nekk?" asked Tonton. "Ci yoon bii?" Awa directed him into a medina with dirt streets and crumbling concrete walls. As Tonton swung the jeep around a sharp curve, the sacked chicken bounced into my lap and I screamed. Tonton and Awa laughed until we slammed to a stop in front of a blue gate.

Awa got out in a wave of orange gauze and went over to the old man, probably a guardian, sitting in front of the gate. He sat on his heels, perfectly balanced, with his arms folded elegantly in his lap. I could see the skeleton beneath his leathery skin. As Awa spoke, she moved her arms, fluttering the sleeve of her bright *boubou* against his tattered gray robe. Whatever she said to him in Wolof made him grin toothlessly and bob his bald head up and down.

After a short silence, Tonton grinned at me and said, "Attention au poulet." He nodded at the chicken thrashing in its sack. "It will eat you!" He laughed loudly, then lit a cigarette. "Mais, pourquoi est-ce que tu vas au marabout? Est-ce que tu veux faire le maraboutage contre ton copain?"

"No, I'm not going to do *maraboutage* against my boyfriend," I said. "I'm going to ask the *marabout* to make me stop drinking."

"Ah, bon." He obviously thought I was lying and asked me again what kind of evil I meant to bring on the man who had just left me.

"No evil," I said.

"That's good. These Senegalese women run to a *marabout* as soon as their men make a mistake, and boom! You see, they have no patience. You need only ask the *Conja* man for patience, not for evil *gris-gris*. With patience, you can have anything you want." He repeated the Wolof proverb "Ndank, ndank mooy japp golo ci ñaay," which means: "Slowly, slowly, the hunter catches the monkey in the woods."

"What are you waiting in here for?" asked Awa, opening the back of the jeep. "Are you two eating our rooster?" As I climbed out, she handed me the sack, saying, "Now hold it like this, by its feet, so the blood will go to its head and keep it stunned. I don't want to hear you scream."

Tonton drove off in the chariot, and I fell into Awa's wake. She led me through the gate, onto a sandy path that wound through a maze of shacks. "Asalaa maalekum," she called out until a little boy led us to a green door, knocked, and ran away.

"Hello, are you fine?" Conté asked in English. He shook our hands and led us into a room lit by a candle stub in a Coke bottle. "Excuse me, but the current is off today. You can see, I hope?" He motioned for us to sit on the mat. Then he lit another candle, tilted it so that the wax ran down the side, and pressed it against the concrete wall until it stuck. He looked young — no older than twenty, and I was disappointed. He wore a faded Salvation Army T-shirt printed with a picture of Miss Piggy and Kermit. As he sat down cross-legged on the mat, he slid on a pair of horn-rimmed glasses that had no lenses in the frames.

"Cigarette?" he asked. I took one from the pack he pulled out of a goatskin bag and smoked while he and Awa talked to each other in Creole. They were both from Freetown, and they greeted each other like long-lost cousins before they settled down to the business of haggling.

"Sister, wha' you say? Me bad thin' or good thin'?" The *Conja* man looked pained.

"Yes, man," Awa said, her eyes glowing, "you good thin'. You good thin' but you no see."

I looked around the room. The furniture consisted of a double mattress and a dresser covered with dishes. A suit of clothes in a plastic bag hung on the wall, which was painted sky blue. The floor was covered with blue linoleum, and the corner behind Conté was curtained off with a ratty piece of red velvet. The chicken was so quiet in its sack that I wondered if I had accidentally killed it.

"I'd like two *gris-gris,*" I said. Neither of the Sierra-Leonians paid any attention to me.

Conté leaned forward, stretching out his hands, and said something to Awa. She put her hand to her throat and rolled her eyes up to the ceiling as she groaned. Then she clicked her tongue; he did the same. The candles flickered. The two of them argued until the candle stub burned down into the Coke bottle. When Conté rose to light another one, Awa turned to me, very businesslike, and quoted his prices.

"The basic reading is two thousand C.F.A.," she said. "Protection for travel — he says you are going on a trip — will be five thousand. That covers land, air, and sea. If you want a *gris-gris* for love, that will be another six thousand." I frowned at her and shook my head.

"She no wan' love," Awa said.

Conté stood next to the candle and widened his eyes. "Wha'?" He removed his glasses and looked down at me. "Why she no wan' love?"

She no good at it, I thought. Awa glanced at me. "Can you set ice on fire?" I asked. I had heard tales of *marabouts* doing this but had never seen it performed. Today, explained Conté, he did not have the special ingredients to set fire to ice, but he would be happy to do this for me another day. He reached behind the red velvet curtain and pulled out what he did have today: a small wooden statue of a man with breasts, a Koran, and several packets of powders. "I want two *gris-gris,*" I said. "One to make me a social drinker, and one to give me patience. How much will that cost?"

He looked at the statue. "Five thousand."

"Four thousand five hundred."

He sighed. "I have expenses," he said. "I must buy the herbs to make the *gris-gris,* you see."

"I am not rich," I said. "I am a Peace Corps volunteer."

"I must pay rent."

"I understand, but I have no money either."

"I must send money to my mother."

"This is true."

"You pay four thousand five hundred seventy-five," he said. "C'est mon dernier prix." As we shook hands, I realized that we had been quibbling over the equivalent of a dollar and a half. I hated bargaining. If I got the price I wanted, I felt guilty, and if I didn't get it, I felt cheated. Even though another American had once assured me that when Americans deal with Africans, we always lose, I was taken in, again and again, by the sighs, shrugs, and downcast eyes.

Conté needed a piece of paper. He spent several minutes shuffling around behind the red velvet curtain; then he went through all the drawers in his dresser. I looked at my watch. He finally came up with a used envelope. "Now we are ready," he said, smiling triumphantly as he sat down in front of me. Then he remembered that he needed a pencil.

"I must go out and borrow one," he said, smiling pleasantly at Awa and me. "I will be back shortly." I gritted my teeth.

Awa removed a pencil from her pocket and handed it to him.

He wrote my name in Arabic on the back of the envelope. Then he took the cock out of the sack, lifting it with both hands, and began to chant. The words made a hollow, sad sound. He chanted as he handed the bird first to Awa, then to me. I held it against my chest, pressing my fingers into the warm red and gold feathers beneath the wings, the way Awa had done. I felt the heart pulse. "He's showing you that the rooster is alive," said Awa. "Think of the first thing you want. Think hard."

All I could think was, *I want a bourbon and Coke.* As I pressed my fingers into the warm feathers, I tried to think, *I want to be a social drinker.* I tried to think, *I want patience,* but the harder I concentrated, the more I wanted a bourbon and Coke. I could taste the sweet whiskey and feel it burn down my throat, warm my belly. My arms trembled as I handed the cock back to Conté, who was still chanting.

He pressed his fingers beneath the chicken's wings, chanting faster and faster. The bird's black eyes turned glassy and began to blink. It shuddered, once, twice, then it blinked its eyes again, refusing to die. Conté chanted wildly. He sat cross-legged, as still as the rooster, and like the rooster he blinked his eyes as though struggling to remain awake. The air in the small, dark room rang with Arabic. Suddenly the cock shook violently. This time its eyes stayed shut. Conté held it, chanting softly, until the neck dropped and went limp. Then he handed the bird to me.

"He wants you to hold it and see that it is dead," said Awa, "before he brings it back to life."

I took the warm, dead cock in my hands. Its neck hung down like a piece of rubber, but the red comb was still bright and stiff.

"Yes," I said. "It's dead. I see."

Then something went wrong. Conté called out to the spirits until he was hoarse, until the candles burned down and we were sitting in the dark, but he could not resurrect the chicken.

"This a bad thin'," he said, setting the dead bird on the floor.

"There's something evil in the room," said Awa. I tried to act surprised. "Someone has done something," she said, looking my way as I bent forward to tie my shoe. "Someone has blocked the spirit."

"This a bad thin'," Conté said again. "This no good."

I wanted a drink so badly that my scalp crawled. It seemed like we would never get out of that room and get to a bar, but finally Awa and Conté finished saying goodbye to each other. I gave Conté a five-thousand C.F.A. note.

"Wait," he said, when he had turned his pockets out and found them empty.

"It's okay."

"No, wait." I waited while he went through his dresser looking for four hundred twenty-five C.F.A. "I will go ask my friend," he said at last.

"Never mind. Keep the change."

"You come here tomorrow," he said, smiling, "and I will have this other *gris-gris* made for you, the one for patience."

We shook hands and he walked us back through the maze of houses and part of the way down the street. It was a Senegalese custom to walk a guest not just to the door, but a good way along his path; sometimes a host accompanied his guest all the way home. I couldn't wait for Conté to turn back so I could duck into a bar, but Awa was hungry, so we went into a *dibiterie*.

We ordered plates of meat from a butcher standing beneath a ceiling of skinned lambs whose rubbery legs were pulled taut, exposing the bellies. "Asseyez," he said, slicing a knife through the air, and we sat on a bench at a low wooden table.

"I can't remember the last time I ate," I said, watching the rise and fall of the knife in the butcher's hand. Awa looked at me as if she would prefer I starved to death. "I'm sorry," I said.

When the butcher brought our food, we ate it with our hands, sucking the grease off our fingers. The butcher nodded at us and smiled.

"Neexul," he said. "It must be terrible."

"Déedéet," I said. "Neex na. It's good!"

"Lekkal. Eat more."

"Sur nañu," said Awa. "We're full."

After we ate, we walked down the street into a bar lit by a blue light bulb. Awa went ahead of me, pushing apart the strips of colored plastic that hung from the door, and when they fell back across my shoulders, I saw Conté. He was drinking a glass of milk at the bar while he fiddled with a broken transistor radio.

"Hello, my sisters!" he cried. "Are you fine?" While he ordered the man behind the counter to bring us drinks on the house, he led us to a table as if he owned the bar. For a second, not wanting to hurt Conté's feelings, I considered ordering a Coke. However, I reasoned, the chicken was dead, and drinking Coke wouldn't bring it back to life. Awa asked for one of the airplane bottles of Hennessy on the shelf behind the cash register and I ordered a Coke and an airplane bottle of Jack Daniels.

Conté smiled. After he made sure that we were comfortable, he ambled back to the bar and began to flirt with a young girl who wore her hair in a new style called the baobab. According to legend, the baobab tree had once been the most beautiful tree in Senegal, but it grew vain, so God turned it upside down, burying the lovely branches beneath the ground and sticking the ugly roots up in the sky. With twenty or thirty short braids poking out all over her head, the girl did look something like a baobab tree.

"I have come to this," Awa said. "I am drinking in front of my *marabout.*"

"He doesn't seem to mind," I said. The girl squealed and slapped his hand as he pretended to slide her *boubou* away from her shoulder.

"You don't understand," Awa said. "This man is powerful. What am I doing talking to a Brownie?"

"You're educating me." Sweat dripped down our necks and I ordered another round.

"Do you know what you said to me last night, sweetness?"

"Don't tell me."

"When I had my shoes off, ready to rescue you from drowning, you popped your pointed little head out of the water and said —" She paused and cleared her throat. On Sundays Awa preached at the Methodist church, and when she drank, she practiced her King James voice on me. "You said — and mind you were talking to me, Awa — you said, 'Oh, Miss.'"

I stared into my drink.

"'Oh, Miss,' you called from the deep end, 'bring me a bourbon and Coke.' When I didn't dash to the bar to serve you — here you are drowning and I'm the only fool in the place who can swim — you instructed me to send you the drink out on a tray. The cork-lined trays, you explained, would float."

"Was Yousouf there?"

"Oh, it was brilliant, sweetness. I should have charged admission."

"Was he?"

"No." She lit a cigarette, then shook her head and said in a low voice, "Làmmiñ baaxul. The tongue is bad." The waiter brought us more airplane bottles, and from across the room, Conté nodded. *Marabouts* have certain privileges in their neighborhoods; apparently we could drink all night on the house. When Awa got drunk, she began to talk about a man she called "he."

"To give you an example of how brilliant people are," she said, "men are slower than women of course, and slower than all of the other animals; that's just the time it takes them to realize what is happening — but brilliance!"

"I'm losing you."

"Of course you are. I'm talking about psychological manipulation. Once someone called our house and no one answered the phone. I was listening to the stereo on headphones, so I didn't hear the phone ring. It was *his* family calling. They came directly to the house to tell *him* that they had just called and no one picked up the phone. Do you know what *he* said?"

I shook my head and poured more bourbon in my Coke.

"He said, 'She does that. I watched her sit right next to the phone without answering it. She does that on purpose.' It took these people three days to realize that if *he* had been watching me not answer the phone then *he* also must have heard the phone ring."

Later, when the empty airplane bottles were lined up on the table and the walls were sliding, she said, "I saw him at the grocery store the other day. He wanted to say hello. He was standing in front of the spice rack. When he saw me, he took two steps forward and opened his mouth . . . I could see that his mouth was trying to say hello. He tried. His lips moved, but he just couldn't say the word." She had been leaning forward with her elbows on the table, staring intently into my face, and now she sat back. "I find that sad, don't you?"

"You're crazy," I said, but I meant me.

"Then you're crazy to be with me," she said. "Aren't you?"

I looked away. The girl with the baobab hairdo was kissing our *marabout.* I had drunk past the point of pleasure, but I couldn't stop; I was on the edge of what I called the black hole. In the black hole, I'd Maced a lover, kicked in windows, hit people, stolen. When I came to, I would try to explain to Yousouf that the girl who did these things was not me, not really.

Suddenly I thought about the night before, lying on the black and white tiles of my living room floor with an empty bottle of Four Roses and my army knife. I had a plan, I explained to Yousouf. I was going to cut off the pinkie of my right hand so that the next time I picked up a drink I would remember that when I drank, I did things like cut off my fingers. He couldn't follow my train of thought because I was a genius. I called him stupid.

"Yes, Awa," I said, "I'm crazy. Let's get out of here."

Outside, a pale moon shone through a sickly tree by the road. A leper called out, "Madame! Donne-moi cent francs!" His fingers looked like they had grown back into his hands. When he waved at us, he cried out with horrible cheerfulness, "Au revoir, Madame!"

"I wonder what it would feel like to see yourself growing back into yourself every day," I said. "Would it be like growing up backwards?"

"You don't understand," Awa said. "He's not here. Nobody is here, Darren. He only speaks to you because you are a *ñak*, a goat, a foreigner; he knows that you *think* you are here." She stepped out and waved at a taxi but it passed us by, so we continued to walk.

When we came to a shop where men were making shoes, we both stopped. Their light flooded out into the dark street, and I could smell the clean air around them as I watched them work. One of them sliced leather while the other one tapped it onto freshly carved soles. On the wall behind them, pointed yellow shoes, each decorated with a different design in black Magic Marker, hung in pairs.

"I want that," I said.

"I know," Awa said. For a second she rested her hand on my shoulder; then she swung away to hail a cab.

The next morning Rokhaya let herself in with her key. When she saw me lift my head off the pillow, she called out, "Asalaa maalekum," and brought me a beer, a glass of water, and two aspirin. "Na nga def?" she asked sweetly. She had a new hairdo — the baobab — and she was wearing my Mickey Mouse T-shirt.

"Maa ngi fii rekk," I grumbled, reaching for the water. In many respects, Yousouf had good reason to complain about our maid. Though she was a good cook, she flatly refused to prepare certain dishes. "Chicken livers will make you a coward," she told me, and that was that. She used my makeup, constantly borrowed money, and burned clothes so badly that I had to take the iron away from her. Yousouf said that this was her intention.

As soon as Yousouf was out of earshot, she called him El Hadji Mor, which translates roughly as Mr. Big Shot, or *borom kër,* the head of the house. We both suspected that she pretended not to understand a word of French so she could eavesdrop.

Despite these faults, Rokhaya was the perfect maid for me. She never let me run out of beer. Every day she marched down to the Lebanese *épicerie* to replenish my stock, and when the other maids in the building complained that it was unseemly for a Muslim woman to be seen handling so much alcohol, she explained that white people need beer the way black people need water. Privately she told me that the other maids were all whores. In any case, I couldn't get rid of her. She had laid claim to me when I first came to the country, and though she had grudgingly forgiven me for refusing to call myself Rokhaya, she would never understand how I could put her out of work after hiring her away from her job with the Peace Corps training camp in Thiès.

"Ana borom kër gi?" she asked as she pulled a basket of clean, wrinkled clothes from the closet and began to fold them on the foot of my bed.

"Dem na," I said. "He's gone."

"Fan la dem?"

I drank some beer and pointed out the window.

"Dem na rekk?" She lifted her head from the basket and pretended to be horrified. "Laay i laay! Lutax?"

"Xamuma." I shrugged. "I don't know why." When I finished the beer, she brought me another one, and I gradually told her the whole story: the swimming pool incident, the note, my failed encounter with Conté the *Conja* man. She was rapt, crying out "Laay i laay" at every opportunity and asking questions to make sure she got the story exactly right.

"The friend who saved you, what's her name?"

"Awa."

"Waaw, waaw." She held up a pair of my socks. "Séex," she

said. "Awa." She waved the socks in my face and then I understood. She meant that Awa was my twin.

"Yes, she's my twin."

"This is a good woman," she said. "This is a good friend. You must have *gris-gris*. El Hadji Mor doesn't want you to have any *gris-gris* because men are afraid of women's power. This has been the case since time began." She patted my foot. "Ignore it, *patronne.*"

"Do you think Yousouf will come back?"

"Ah, bien sûr." She frowned. "He will be back."

"When?"

"When, when, when? You have no patience. If you had called yourself Rokhaya, I think you would have more patience. Rokhaya is patient." I sighed, and she patted me on the head.

That afternoon I took a cab back to Conté's house to get my *gris-gris* for patience, but the old man at the gate said he wasn't home.

"He will be back soon, very soon," he assured me. "Sit and wait."

"Jëre-jëf waay," I said, smiling and shaking his hand. "Ba suba."

He nodded. "Tomorrow," he repeated. "Ba suba."

The next day I found Conté at home, but he had not yet made the *gris-gris*. He told me to come back the next day at three o'clock, which I did, but again the guardian told me that he wasn't home.

"Ba suba."

"Waaw, waaw," I said. "I'll come tomorrow," but I gave up and never went back for the *gris-gris*.

I didn't really want patience anyway; I spent those three days taking cabs to and from Conté's house to avoid thinking about Yousouf. The apartment seemed smaller without him. I spread some of his clothes around on the chairs to make it look like he still lived there, but Rokhaya put them all away. Once or twice I played some of his music, but he liked Baba Maal and Barbra Streisand; even when I missed him, I hated his tapes.

Then one night he walked in the door. He had gotten a haircut; his ears looked vulnerable. "Bonsoir," he said formally. "Comment ça va?"

"Stay," I said.

"No."

"Forgive me."

"You insult me."

"I promise, I will never insult you again."

"You have promised before," he said, but he took two steps closer to me.

I breathed deeply. If he kissed me, he was mine again. He crossed his arms over his chest, but he was looking me in the eye. "I told myself that this was the last time I ever am with you," he said. "I made this promise to myself and God. Some people do not break promises." I turned my eyes down and waited.

"Did you go with your friend Awa to get a *gris-gris* against me?" he asked. "I think this is what you have done because I am standing here against my will. I cannot love you if you do not change. I have thought about this. I am doing everything for you, thinking, here is this American woman, and I do not want to lose her. Eh, *Boy?* Look to me." I looked into his eyes, wanting to touch him, but I waited. "I am not doing no more dishes," he said. "I would ask you to stop drinking, but I know that you would choose the Flag beer over me. N'est-ce pas?"

I shook my head.

"Yes, it's true. So you can drink, but when you are drunk, you will go to sleep and not fight me or I will leave. Really, I will. Do you understand?"

After we made love, he stretched his arms behind his head and said, "You know, your friend Awa has a broken neck."

"Heart," I said. I touched my chest.

"Yes, a broken heart."

"Who broke her heart?"

"A Senegalese man, *bien sûr.*" He smiled and touched my breast. "He was a politician traveling in New York City. They fell in love and married. I think they were very happy in the United States, but he did not explain the Senegalese practice of polygamy. When he brought her back to Dakar, she found that he had forgotten to tell her he had one wife and some children here. I think she must be very angry with this man."

"When did she divorce him?"

"She is still married to him."

"No!" I sat up. "That's her ex-husband."

"Ah, bon? But you see, he is a customer at my bank, and he tells me that she will not give him the divorce. This is what I do not understand. It is very sad. He tells me that she was pregnant with twins when he brought her back to Africa, and they died inside of her."

"Yousouf, I've been to her house. She doesn't have a husband. Awa is a strong woman. She wouldn't tolerate being a second wife."

"This is what I am thinking, but I tell you the truth. She does not live with him, but it is seven years now, and she will not divorce him. She is stubborn, but she is weak with love. How do you say in English — love is blind?"

I rolled over on my stomach and rested my chin in my hands. I wanted a smoke, but he hated me to smoke in bed. "Do you think I'm strong?" I asked him. All of my former lovers had paused in their extensive criticisms of my character to admit that I was a strong woman.

"Non," he said. "Tu n'es pas forte."

"I'm not strong?"

"No, you are not strong." He slid his hand along my thigh. "You have strong legs, and you have a strong intelligence, but you are not a strong person, inside."

"I hate weak people," I said.

"I don't. I like weak people."

He began to speak to me in his native tongue, Mandinka. I didn't understand a word. I moved my head onto his chest, and before long I fell asleep with his arms around me.

In the middle of the night I woke up. I was sober, and I didn't like the sensation. I crept into the kitchen, but before I turned on the light, I remembered that I was out of beer. Time seemed to stop. I sat down in the middle of the living room floor, in the same place I had lain when I decided to cut off one finger. A few minutes later Yousouf came into the room, rubbing his eyes.

"Qu'est-ce qu'il y a?"

"I'm sober," I said.

"C'est bon."

"No, it's not good." My voice quivered, and then I began to cry, trying to make him come close to me and touch me, but he stayed across the room, watching.

"Qu'est-ce qu'il y a, Darren?"

"It's the hole."

"Your black hole?"

"Help me."

"I can't do nothing." His voice was hoarse with sleep, and I wondered if he was even awake. Sometimes he walked in his sleep. "Even when I make love to you, this hole is empty. Even if I put a child in your belly, you will have this hole."

"What should I do?"

"Maybe this hole is supposed to be in you. Maybe you should not try to fill it up. Maybe this is the place God saves for himself."

"God is not in my black hole!"

"You do not even give God time. Ndank, ndank, Boy. Slowly, slowly." He came forward, took my hand, and led me back to the bed.

While he slept with his head under the covers, I lay beside him with my eyes wide open. The hole grew deeper and wider; and then it began to hurt. It hurt so much I knew I couldn't live, but I couldn't die, either. Finally, I prayed, *Lord God, you bastard, help me.*

A FOOL IN LOVE

Hello. Na nga def? Ça va? I like your teeth. Give them to me.
You are walking. I will join you. For some of us, it is an effort
to be rude, n'est-ce pas? We had good home training, as you say
in Tennessee. I was born here in Dakar, in the telephone booth
on Rue de Thon, Tuna Fish Street. My mother is the sky, and my
father is a pig. I won't bore you with the details of my childhood.
You are lost. I sympathize. Je te manque, tu me manques; you
are missing me, I am missing you. Eh, Fatou? Cat got your
tongue?

Turning a corner, so coy. Really, Mademoiselle, your legs are
short. C'est très amusant. Pardon?

Oh, a nasty word! I have hurt your feelings. Are you afraid to
look at me in the dark? Slow down. Regarde-moi. You don't
remember me?

They call me the fool — by mistake. He's a fucking horror!

Don't confuse me with that idiot. I am a genius, like you. Call me Bopp. If I am the part of me I cannot see, I'd rather be a head than an ass.

Nude? How clever of you to notice. I love my clothes, but they are unfaithful. When I turn my head, a flip-flop flaps away, leaving a mate who leaves me too. Shirts tear off in tantrums. Hats fly south. My beloved drawers creep down my legs and slip away in the night. Everything gets lost. Are you lost, ma petite? *You don't live around here. You are afraid I will follow you home, vain woman, but look, you have followed me home. This is Rue de Thon. My residence takes up the entire street, from our wedding-cake palace that makes me so hungry to the dirty little bakery where I eat. Welcome, Darren.* Fais comme chez toi.

Shall we discuss sex, politics, or religion? You hate my city. Yes, the demons hump like rats and multiply, and it's true that the air smells of piss and rotting goat, but all of this will change. Everything changes, praise Allah.

Sit, Fatou, don't be a snob. Dirtier things than my curb have felt your ass. There's that nasty word again. Touchy, aren't we? Toogal waay. If you try to get away, I'll kill you. Now, sit beside me, chérie, *and relax. We will confide in each other like friends.*

Yesterday, I fell in love. I have been miserable ever since. She's a baby blue Lincoln Continental, ooo-AMG. *Isn't that an American embassy license plate? Of course you don't know, my friend; you are afraid, so you wander about with your eyes shut. Thus, you are lost.*

I watch everything. For some time now, I've watched my baby circling La Place de l'Indépendence, a bluebird trapped in a line of shiny black roaches, around and around the palace they go — ta, ta de da. But yesterday, Fatou, she broke away, swept down Rue de Thon, and screeched to a halt right in front of me.

Excuse-moi? Was I the only naked fool standing in the street? I assure you, Mademoiselle, she stopped for me. Give me a cigarette. I do believe you are jealous. She parked right here where we are sitting and purred at me. She was spanking clean, as usual. Her jewels threw light into my face. At first I was ashamed of my nakedness, but my po-po *rose to greet her and, well, she honked. When I petted her behind, she farted, but even that was endearing.* Mon dieu, *I am in love! I am losing my mind.*

Really, your sarcasm doesn't affect me. Sit. I have not finished my story. We are coming to the scary part. Oh, you're not so brave. Yaaah! Aha!

Forgive me. You are trembling. Doucement, doucement. *I apologize.* Je m'excuse. *Please don't scream; it makes your face so ugly. May I continue?*

Thank you. As I was saying, I caressed her. She responded. I was very happy. Excited. Titillated. Comprends? *Well, suddenly, she shook all over, and something disgusting crawled out of her belly — a big, fat, white demon. He waved his fist and shouted obscenities at me. His clothes clung to him as if frightened for their lives.*

"Hey!" *the demon yelled.* "Get out of here! Va-t'en!"

I was not afraid. Do you see these grìs-grìs *tied into my hair? They are so powerful that even I don't know what they mean, but when I shake my head, my enemies flee.* "Yaah!" *I yelled. I waved my arms, stomped my feet, and shook my head until the talismans banged against my skull and gave me a terrible headache.* "Gaarrr!" *I roared. A confession, between us: while my head clacked out a glorious hymn to God, my mind sat like a manioc root.*

Pardon, Fatou; even geniuses forget to think. I had intended to rescue ooo-AMG *from her demon, but instead of running down the street, he naturally shrank back whence he'd come, into her belly. It was I who finally ran down the street, and this is all due to the curse of love. Of course I went after my lover's parasite, but when I bent down to pull him out of her belly, I saw a flash of light, then the fool. He was enormous. His red eyes rolled. Foam flecked his snapping mouth. He had the balls of a donkey and a* po-po *nearly as large as my own. As he twisted his thick neck, I saw things falling out of his head. When I screamed, he screamed back, and I fled.*

I ran behind the bakery, down an alley, past the grills of sizzling brochettes and across Avenue Pompidou, to the cool green garden in front of L'Ambassade Américaine, where I rolled under a tree. I lay there with my chest beating like a drum, and all I could think was, She is gone. *It was as if a part of me had flown away. When I looked up at the sky, I saw only clouds. "Maman!" I called. She did not answer. I knew what was coming next. One of the clouds turned into a floating white pig. "Ayca! I wasn't talking to you," I said. "Bëg naa suma yaay. I want my mother."*

The pig said, "So sorry." Then it bared its genitals at me and cackled.

Are you following me, Fatou? I have noticed that you always must have something in your hand. You hold a drink or some bread or a cigarette or Mace or a knife or a man. Look, right now you are holding a rock. Busy, busy, little American. Are you afraid that you might fall off the earth if you don't hold on? Let go, my friend. You must drop the rock if you want to hear the end of my story.

The guards began to come toward me, your American embassy guards, but they are Senegalese of course, bien adaptés au climat. I ignored them, got on my knees, and began to pray. I do not pray these long dirges you hear all around the mosques on Fridays when the demons sport their grand boubous. Yàlla this, Yàlla that. Yàlla I cannot get off my knees because I am so fat. You've heard these groans, and still you have not converted to Islam? Stubborn Fatou!

I offered my humble prayer: Help. Then the guards stopped

in their path, the pig turned back into a cloud, and God dropped
three tiny, crisp, light pastries down from heaven. They were pink
and yellow and they fluttered around my hand until I ate them,
one butterfly, two butterfly, three . . .
  Yaa ngiy dem? You are leaving? You want to get drunk, fall in
love, wear a crown and eat Le Palais du Président? Come back
again, Fatou-Darren. Don't be a stranger.

The riot began with a group of high school boys running around
the palace at La Place de l'Indépendence and into the narrow Rue
de Thon, raising the cry "Sopi!" which means change. Somehow they swept up everything in their path: a mailman with a
Republic of Senegal bag swinging from his shoulder; two wiry
boys who clutched half-eaten loaves of bread and sprinted, shirt-
tails flying; and Darren, who had not read the Peace Corps
notice warning volunteers to stay out of Dakar that afternoon.
  She had been having cocktails at a French bar on the Place,
and she was dressed up. She wore a long batik skirt, a white
cotton T-shirt, her cowboy boots, and a vest she had ordered
from Around the World because she liked the description:

> This vest may get you into trouble. People will think you
> smoke, drink, gamble, tie or untie women to railroad tracks.
> On the other hand, men aren't itching to fight with you, and
> women may throw themselves in front of oncoming trains for
> you — you rescue her, of course, and then take her to dinner
> at the Ritz (the gambling does pay off, after all). Sorry, one size
> does not fit all. But it may fit you.

Mentally she had substituted "women" for "men," and she had
ordered a men's XL, so that the vest swung off her shoulders
when she walked. It was her favorite piece of clothing.
  Now, as the crowd came down on her and she had to run in

order not to be run over, the heavy slap of suede against her back gave her courage. When she passed a woman crying "Sopi!" as she trotted with one arm behind her back to keep her baby from jostling, Darren wondered if this woman, or any of these rebels, knew that the leader of the Sopi party had been thrown in jail. Feeling like one of the original rioters, Darren imagined that she had entered the protest on purpose. The mob swelled in the narrow lane, forcing the gendarmes flat back against the storefronts. They stood with stony faces and gripped billy clubs.

One of the gendarmes reached out to grab a boy sailing along the edge of the crowd, but an arm knocked the pointed green cap off his head and he had to jump back against the wall as the handsome headpiece with its official red badge was crushed under a thousand stamping feet. "Sopi! Sopi! Sopi!" chanted the mob. Then, from around the corner, behind the bakery, came the fool.

He was nearly eight feet tall. In his rat's nest of dreadlocks he had tied small blocks of wood that clacked together as he walked. Otherwise he was as naked as Adam. When he first came around the side of the bakery, he did not seem to notice the riot. He was looking up at the sky, arguing plaintively. "Lutax?" he asked. "Why?" Then he shook his fist at a cloud and cursed. Suddenly a light seemed to cross his face, and he turned to the crowd stampeding past him. He smiled. He began to clap his hands, chanting, "Sopi, sopi, sopi!" A moment later he wandered off behind the bakery.

When he returned, he was dressed in ragged underwear and one tennis shoe. In this suit he paced back and forth along the curb. He shouted encouragements to the mob as if it were his soccer team. "Sopi!" he screamed. "Change, change, change!" He jumped up and down until the blocks of wood on his head clacked together. He made terrible faces. At one point he grew so excited that tears ran down his cheeks. Then, unable to bear his passion alone, he jumped into the crowd and began to run.

"Sopi!" he shouted joyfully. Being a fool, he ran the wrong way. He ran toward the Place de l'Indépendence, against the mob. He hurtled himself into the people as if they would part around him like water. Twice he was flattened and twice he rose up and ran again, clamoring for change. When he fell for the third time, he landed at the gleaming black boots of a gendarme.

"Sopi!" he cried as he rose to his full height, a head taller than the gendarme, who immediately whacked him with his billy club. The fool looked to the mob for help, but they ran on without him.

"Ayca!" ordered the gendarme. Again he cracked him across the head with his stick. Dazed, the fool stepped back. For a moment, he looked almost sane.

"Change," he told the gendarme.

"Dof!" cried the soldier, and he began to beat him. The fool staggered, regained his balance, and sputtered.

"Sopi! Sopi!"

A few people in the crowd slowed down to watch the beating. Gradually, people stopped running to see what was happening. The cry of "Sopi" diminished into a general buzz; the mob slackened. Then one boy kicked the fool. A loose, electric energy ran through the crowd, now shifting aimlessly under the hot sun. When a man, who must have thought the fool was fighting the boy, or perhaps thought nothing at all, began to beat him, others did the same, knocking the fool to the ground as he begged for change.

An hour later, when they left him bleeding in the street, Darren edged toward him. He was red with blood but his chest moved up and down, and nothing but perhaps his nose appeared to be broken. He had lost his underwear, but he was still wearing his tennis shoe. "Ça va?" she asked. He didn't answer. While some children hooted across the street, she rummaged in a pile of garbage until she found a broomstick. "Here," she said, setting the cane near his massive hand, "use this to stand up." He groaned. "If you don't use this stick to pick yourself up off the ground," she said, "somebody is going to come along and use it to kill you. Society being what it is. People being the apes in clothes that they are. Worse than apes. Demons, like you said." She had begun to cry.

"Toubab!" called one of the children. The others snickered.

"Oh, shut up before I tell your father to beat you!" said Darren. She glared at the boy, who made a face but didn't say another word. Then she prodded the fool with the broomstick. "Hey, get up! Dresse-toi! I'm not going to stand here all day and wait for you to get well." She didn't know why she was crying until she remembered a message she had read on a bathroom wall. She could not remember the quote exactly, but she thought it might have been: *When one human being loses his dignity, for that moment the entire human race has lost its dignity.* A coat was mentioned: *Then you must give him your coat.* Or was it: *When you give him your coat, you restore dignity to the entire human race.*

Well, I don't have a coat, she thought, touching the saloon red satin lining of her vest. She fingered a tagua nut button. The vest had cost one hundred and sixty-seven dollars plus tax and shipping. The fool would get it dirty and probably lose it in ten minutes. God only knew; he might try to eat it and choke to death.

"Hey," she said, poking him with the broomstick. When he opened his eyes and took the crutch, she tossed her vest at him and ran away.

I'm stumbling home one night in the rain, drunk, when I hear a shrill "Fatou! Oh, na nga def, Fatou? Ça va?"

"Hello, Fool," I say to myself, and walk faster.

"Sss . . . Mademoiselle," he hisses, and here he comes on his broomstick, hobbling instead of flying. The stick goes tap, tap, tap, and he swings up beside me, my Adonis. He's wearing my vest and one tennis shoe, which he has chosen to put on his injured foot, the one that doesn't touch the ground. "Fatou! Hello, my friend. Are you fine?"

"Peachy keen," I say, swerving around him.

"You are drunk!" He squeals. "Ha, ha, Fatou-Darren, you walk like a crab."

The rain comes down in sheets, plastering my hair over my eyes. Whenever I get my hair done, we have a hurricane. "Ayca," I say. "Go away." He is ruining my vest in this rain.

"I like your haircut. C'est très mignon, ça." He hops closer to get a better look at me. "Mademoiselle, je t'aime."

Should I run? Will he chase me? Will he slip and fall on the wet pavement? I resolve not to look at him, but when I do I see the raindrops caught in his fright wig; they sparkle under the streetlamp like tiny diamonds. Rain streams down his face, his arms, his naked chest. "I love you, Darren-Fatou," he says, tapping along beside me on the broomstick.

"I thought you loved a car," I say.

"I don't remember saying that."

Men. "That's because you're an idiot," I say. "You're the fool, you know. You see yourself in the mirror and say it's someone else, but you know that it's you."

"Words are only a way for us to be together," he says. "Pig-in-the-blanket."

"Excuse me, but we are not together."

"Eau de javel," he says. "Fu nekk. Forklift. Kangaroo saloon."

"Who are you?"

"Don't you know me? I am the anti-poet."

"Bayyi ko ba beneen yoon," I say. "Until our paths meet again."

"Laaylaay, toubab bi dégg na Wolof!" he says. "Good Lord, this white person speaks Wolof!"

The fool stays on my path. In Senegal, he says, only crazy people walk alone.